ASSIMILATION

ASSIMILATION

Sophie Buchaillard

Assimilation: Etymologically derived from the French. The action of making or becoming like; the state of being like; similarity, resemblance, likeness.

(Oxford English Dictionary)

Assimilation is the parasitic lie used to hollow out the migrant, making husks of former selves; complex mosaics reduced to a single language, a single culture, in the name of universality.

(Sophie Buchaillard)

HONNO MODERN FICTION

First published in Great Britain in 2024 by Honno Press
D41, Hugh Owen Building, Aberystwyth University, Ceredigion, SY23 3DY

1 2 3 4 5 6 7 8 9 10

A catalogue record for this book is available from the British Library.

Published with the financial support of the Books Council of Wales.

ISBN 978-1-912905-96-6 (paperback)
ISBN 978-1-912905-97-3 (ebook)
Cover design: Ifan Bates
Text design: Elaine Sharples
Printed by: 4Edge Limited

This is a work of fiction and no resemblance to persons living or dead is intended or implied.

To the invisible women
travelling
between cultures.
I see you.

1. ROOTS

Blue Paper

In my mind, family was always a nomadic clan, with its own mores – peppered with Arabic expressions, the smell of *ras el hanout*, platters of tajines, *keftas*, and *cornes de gazelle*. I never stopped to think about the lives they lived, my ancestors, taking root in large houses tended by indigenous servants. All I retained was a tradition of perpetual movement, sketched in notebooks and travel journals by a network of people held together with pale blue international paper marked *par avion*.

Lisbon

Jean steadied his grip around the flat-ended tweezers, taking care to rest his forearm against the hard mahogany table, before lifting the thin layer of gold into an arc, with such precision it seemed to slow time itself. A single drop of sweat rolled from one eyebrow down the deep crevice of his leathered skin, landing in a splatter on the glass of the magnifying lamp he was using to scrutinise the embossing. He blinked, grabbed a soft cloth off his lap and mopped the lens clean. The wafer of gold shimmered under the fluorescent light as he pressed it down onto the sleeve of tanned red leather cast-off he had wrapped along the spine of the notebook, rubbing his thumbnail gently over the lettering. Once he was satisfied with his work, he placed the tweezers in their box and brushed away the excess gold with a rounded paint brush.

Looking up towards the window of his office at the National Library of Portugal, Jean noticed that the light from outside seemed dimmer than usual. In his mind, Lisbon always shone with a warm orange glow, quite unlike the gunmetal of this muted day. Checking his grandfather's wind-up pocket watch, he calculated that if he left immediately, he would reach the post office before the weekend closure, allowing for the gift to reach Paris in time for his niece's birthday. He wrapped the journal in a sheet of coarse brown paper, secured it with a piece of string and traced the familiar address of his sister Marianne's apartment on the front, with the attention characteristic of his profession.

Paris

The leather-bound journal arrived in time for my eighth birthday. It did not contain a note.

"It is from your uncle Jean," my mother said, quivering in anticipation of my grandmother's disapproving frown, as Bonne-Maman presided over the unwrapping of presents with the legitimacy of someone accustomed to the Louis XIV chair.

I turned the book several times in my hands, running my finger along the engraved title that bore my name, finally opening it onto an empty page of thick-grained orange paper. "It is empty," I remarked, puzzled.

The journal had the feel and look of the notebooks my grandfather had shown me, the ones in which he used to record his journeys across Asia and North Africa. They contained a series of observations, illustrated with ink sketches and miniature watercolour paintings. I had delighted in flicking through them when he was still alive, listening to him recall anecdotes like so many travel adventures.

Instantly, I attributed magical properties to the journal, as if somehow it could predict the path my life would take.

"It is a travel journal," my mother clarified, mistaking my silence for incomprehension.

"It is so ... *serious* looking," I replied, running my hand across the embossed golden lettering.

"Uncle Jean made it for you, Charlotte, it is special."

"Why don't you let her open another present, Marianne," my grandmother interrupted. There was no choice in her tone.

I put down the journal, reached for another parcel, a toy iron with its accompanying board wrapped in colourful paper. "That one is from me. A must-have for any young lady," she said.

"Yes, Bonne-Maman. Thank you, Bonne-Maman," I replied with a forced smile.

When my mother came to tuck me into bed that night, I asked why her brother had sent the journal. "I've never even met him," I said.

"Family is a strong bond," my mother replied, patting the journal as if soothing a child. She placed it onto the bedside table, leant forward and kissed my forehead. "Time to sleep." She was smiling at me, yet I detected a hint of sadness at the corners of her lips before she flicked off the switch. I felt her weight rising from the edge of the bed as she straightened the blanket, heard the muffled sound of her footsteps, watched her shadow as it melted into the light of the corridor before the door closed on her.

Lying in darkness, clutching my cuddly bear, I wondered about this mysterious uncle. Jean seldom got a mention, apart from Christmas Day when my mother always made a point of ringing him. She would pass the receiver around the sitting room.

"Remember it is a long-distance call," Bonne-Maman would grumble in crescendo, urging everyone to be succinct. The line was always bad, our voices rebounding along some invisible cable, words delayed into a jumble of meaningless questions and answers. It made me feel awkward, all those eyes staring whilst I obliged, giving a sort of annual report – an A in History; the end of year concert in which I had sang solo in the school choir; the two slices of chocolate *bûche* I had been allowed on Christmas Eve – noteworthy events in the otherwise mundane life of an eight-year-old.

My mother would gesture. "Ask him how he is."

"*On n'a pas à se plaindre*," – nothing to complain about, he would always say; as if his life was a constant.

Family Album

My mother documented every family journey with a small Canon camera. After each trip, she would spend hours dating and labelling the pictures, ordering them into large albums covered in Kraft paper which complemented a collection of albums from the past, records from the many exotic countries our family had passed through.

The oldest picture was dated early 1900s, sepia, showing her grandmother Léonie. Léonie had been born in India, a place called Pondicherry that had been a French settlement since 1674. In the picture, Léonie was immortalised standing in front of the office of the *Banque de l'Indochine* in Hanoi, where her husband had been transferred from Pondicherry. She was wearing a long white dress with laced sleeves tied at the waist with a ribbon. Her hair was gathered in an impossibly tight bun, perched high on top of her head, such that it gave her the look of a missionary's daughter. She couldn't have been more than twenty years old.

In the next picture she stood next to a man in an impeccably tailored white suit, erect with starch and the promise of lucrative trade deals. My great-grandfather. The two of them were framed by Indochinese dignitaries in traditional Vietnamese gowns that I imagined to be brightly coloured, bookended by a battalion of indigenous servants, men of short stature in sombre matching uniforms. Behind them was a large property in the colonial style of the time, white with large windows framed in carved wooden shutters, encased in a covered terrace. The eye guessed at ample wicker *chaises-longues* on which the house inhabitants gathered in the afternoon to chase the heat under large electric fans.

As I scanned the picture, my eye arrested on the light-haired child sat on the lawn.

"Who is that?" I asked my mother.

She pointed at the sticker written in pencil next to the photo. "Helene," she said. "Your grandmother."

Bonne-Maman

The Helene I knew was an elderly woman, stern and principled, who wore her grey hair short like a man's, favoured trousers over skirts, and played board games. Famously, she travelled alone, by car, especially since her husband had passed. In her little Nissan Micra, she continued to take twelve-hour drives well into her eighties on a whim. I'd heard that during the German occupation, when cars were requisitioned to support the war effort, Helene had cycled twelve kilometres a day, my uncle Jean on the luggage rack, and baby Marianne swaddled in the front basket, dropping them off with a local childminder before going to work as a typist in a local factory. After the war ended, I knew that she had divorced from the man whom she had followed to Morocco from Hanoi, a businessman and a *coureur de jupons* – what people in those days referred to as an incurable womaniser. I wasn't certain what had become of the man. My grandfather was the man she had married later. A war surgeon. Of my mother's father I knew nothing, as if the man had somehow been erased from their lives.

In my mother's album, there is a little postcard which Bonne-Maman had sent in 1941 to relatives living under German-occupied France, announcing the birth of her daughter Marianne. At the time, the German administration had printed instructions at the top of such cards: *It is permitted to provide family news, seven lines of text only. It is forbidden to write in between the lines or to give any other type of news. It is essential to write clearly so the content can be controlled by the German authorities.* Looking at the card now, I realise there is a lot more to the experience of those years than what trickled down to my generation through those family albums.

Hanoi

The air was swollen with the promise of monsoon as little Helene stepped out of the imposing white mansion, wrapped in a crisp white pinafore dress, her hand secured into Hue's.

"*Il pleut, il pleut Bergère,*" Helene began to sing, skipping shoulder-to-shoulder with the tiny Vietnamese governess. Together, they walked down the large avenue, along rows of impeccable gardens, tended by armies of invisible hands. One nursery rhyme flowed into another, and another, all the way to the gate of the Lycée Français.

"You have a good day," Hue said, kissing Helene's forehead and handing her a parcel of freshly cooked *nems*, rolled into mint leaves.

"Hurray, hurray," Helene clapped excitedly, before disappearing with her prize into the building.

Hue watched her go, nodding with satisfaction, before heading in the direction of the market to buy provisions for the evening celebration. Madame had sent her with a list, to help the cook who was busy decorating a large birthday cake with swirls of blue icing sugar. Later the cook would need to prepare the meat, but not until Monsieur returned with the hunting party.

The men had left before dawn, with their dogs, their rifles, and their servants, eager to make the most of the last outing before the rainy season. Monsieur would be flanked by his two Royal poodles, and the turbaned attendant he had brought with him from India. The dogs were his pride and joy. Madame had told Helene that the breed was designed to retrieve *canards* – ducks, hence their name of *caniche*. Madame had lamented the way the British had diminished the animals by giving them this ridiculous name of *poodle*. Be they *caniche* or *poodle*, Hue was wary of the dogs. She had heard stories of hounds being set loose on disobedient servants.

The market presented a wide stretch of polychromic spreads hoarding mounds of fleshy vegetables, bright kumquats, and spiky lychees. Farmers stood amongst the monticules, dressed in varied hand-dyed traditional wears, ornate with intricate jewelleries, signifiers of the many tribes from central Vietnam, Laos, and Cambodia who came to Hanoi to sell their products, and had done so long before this part of the world came to be known as Indochina. The market was the only place where Hue sometimes forgot the presence of the French. Their beige costumes and floppy hats seemed countless miles from here.

Walking from stand to stand, she collected the items Madame had listed in her neat handwriting: citrus fruits for the sauce, leafy greens to accompany the *canard à l'orange* Madame had planned for her daughter's eighth birthday. Hue thought that Helene would have preferred caramelised pork ribs and rice eaten in the kitchen amongst the indigenous help, so sticky it could only be eaten with fingers, teeth working their way around the bone, tongue licking at the toffee-coloured glaze. Madame disapproved of course, but the thought made Hue salivate. As she left the market, the weight of her basket made her walk lopsided. Damn *canard à l'orange*, she thought.

Nearing the house, she heard incessant barking and loud exclamations, the words indistinguishable, so that she couldn't tell who was shouting. Past the street corner, she saw a gathering mass, men dressed in light colours coming down from the surrounding houses, men dressed in black appearing from tendered gardens, all with their backs turned, fixated on a small brown form curled at the foot of the mansion's steps. First, Hue noticed the hunting party rallied around Monsieur. Then she saw the turbaned attendant struggling to hold back the crazed dogs. Monsieur raised a hand, commanding silence. The noise died down.

"What is it?" someone asked from the crowd.

"A dog?" someone else hazarded.

Monsieur stepped forward and crouched near what appeared to be a mound of thick fur. What have they killed now, Hue wondered? Monsieur placed his hand on the pelt and Hue registered a ripple, immediately met by the mounting growl of Monsieur's dogs.

10

"Take them away," Monsieur ordered, gesturing in the direction of the turbaned attendant. And then, to the crowd, "This here is a bear cub." He paused, waiting for the murmur carried through the assembly of men to die down. Hue watched as his hand started stroking the animal. There was a shudder, then a little round ear fluttered. Poking his nose up, the miniature bear scanned the air. Monsieur continued to soothe the cub until it unfolded itself, causing the crowd to take a collective intake of breath. The bear sat like a contented Buddha, front paws resting on a rounded belly, observing Monsieur with interest. No taller than Helene, the cub's movements were clumsy, eliciting laughter from the observers.

Questions were asked. Monsieur explained that the hunting party had killed the mother bear. It was a terrible tragedy, he added. "The men found the cub afterwards." He pointed at the dogs. "They were making such a racket. The poor cub had a fright."

"What will you do with him?" someone asked.

"We have the space. We will take care of this *unfortuné*."

Nobody thought to question Monsieur, and after a while, the men just dispersed.

On the way home from the Lycée Français that afternoon, Hue didn't mention the bear to Helene, listening instead to her continuous chattering about the day's history lesson on the French Revolution and the way the People had risen against the royal oppressor.

"They signed *La Déclaration des Droits de l'Homme et du Citoyen* in 1789," Helene told Hue, "So that every man should be born and remain free and equal all of their lives."

Hue wondered why school spent so much time filling the children's heads with such tales instead of teaching them how to cook, clean, and sew, so they wouldn't need to get other people to do it for them.

At home, Madame met Helene's exuberant displays with a stern frown. "Hue, take my daughter to her room to change. The blue dress, the one with little bows." Hue nodded. "And do something about this, this ... mane," Madame said, pointing at her daughter's head. "She looks like a wild beast."

The guests arrived, mostly business colleagues of Monsieur, and a handful of Helene's girlfriends from the Lycée. Everyone was placed by Madame around a long banquet table laid in the garden. Madame said that seating plans required military precision. One wrong placement and some of the *Banque's* dignitaries would feel offended.

Once all were seated, an army of Vietnamese servants in black clothing, impeccably white laced bonnets and matching aprons brought salads, poured wine, cleared the small plates, and presented each guest with a gloriously fragrant plate of *canard à l'orange*, decorated with orange blossom flowers. The meal was a triumph of East meets West, and Madame was filled with a sense of achievement.

At the end of the meal, Madame stood and called Helene to her side. The cook herself wheeled in the cake she had spent all morning decorating with blue icing. A few guests commented on Madame's exquisite attention to detail. Indeed, Helene's ribbons matched the cake to perfection. Madame's chin rose imperceptibly at the acknowledgement.

Coffee was served after the cake. It was Monsieur's turn to rise and call his daughter to his side. With great ceremony, he thanked the assembled guests for their presence, reminding them that it was their funds which allowed the *Banque* to invest in the future of the region. All the while, Helene stood alongside him, back straight, feet parallel, hands behind her back, patiently waiting to play her part. Coming to the end of his speech, Monsieur placed a firm palm onto his daughter's shoulder.

"Today, we are here to celebrate my daughter's birthday." Turning to Helene, he made eye contact and leaned down towards her a little. "We have something special for you dear child." With a sweep of the hand, he directed all eyes towards his turbaned attendant, walking up the garden path pulling something on a rope.

"A bear?" Helene squeaked, forgetting all decorum, looking in turn at the animal waddling towards her, and her father. "Can I?" she asked, running towards the attendant without waiting for an answer. The man lowered his chin and Helene placed her hand onto the cub's head, scratching behind the ears as she had seen her father do with the dogs. The bear nuzzled into her hand.

"Be careful with your dress," Madame said, seeing the mud on the bear.

"There is no need for that," Monsieur appeased her, and to the guests: "I present to you, Arthur, the newest member of our family."

The guests stood in unison and clapped like people did at the military parade of the 14th of July. Behind Monsieur, Helene was rubbing the bear's belly. The bear eyed her attentively, taking in this little girl in her blue dress. She must have looked to him like a fluffy cloud.

Châtellerault

Every year in February, my parents sent me to Bonne-Maman's house during the half-term holiday. Those were special days. She lived on the top floor of a block of flats built in the 1960s, one of those buildings that had sprung from the ground to house families forced to 'return' from the colonies as each declared its independence after the war. From her kitchen window, I remember the view, past the roofs to a grassy hill on which stood a huge oak tree; the place, she told me, where my grandfather was buried. I'll never know why they ended up in that village of the Poitou region my family had no ties to. Maybe simply because the village needed a doctor after the war. Châtellerault's main claim to fame as I was growing up was to have been the place of residence of the first French woman Prime Minister, Edith Cresson. Thanks to her, the Paris–Bordeaux Fast Train stopped in the small town, which meant my parents could simply load me onto the train in Paris with a suitcase and I'd land in my grandmother's arms three hours later.

The memories I have of those week-long holidays are olfactory. The smell of baked brioche and coffee in the morning, the air filled with cumin and saffron as she cooked my favourite: *keftas*, spicy Moroccan meatballs in tomato sauce which we ate from the pot with a large chunk of *kesra*. In the afternoon, we would watch TV together. *Countdown*, *Jeopardy*, and her favourite crime dramas. Huddled on a red velour sofa, surrounded by remnants from all the places where she had lived: a lacquered table decorated with mother of pearl from Indochina, large ceremonial amber necklaces that Bedouins would have worn at fantasias in Morocco, the little statue of a bear, carved in dark wood.

She died during my second year at university. Her instructions said she didn't want to be buried next to her husband since none of us lived locally and we would be unlikely to visit. She was probably right, since now that she was gone, nothing tied us to the town.

Instead, she was cremated. On the day, the man from the funeral parlour invited us to stand in a crescent. We witnessed the moment when he pulled the metal handle from his strange contraption and released her ashes. I remember how the wind picked up, carrying the fine white powder up into the air, forming a rising cloud which, before it dissipated, took on what I would later swear was the shape of a bear.

Another Country

The clamour of voices from the garden alerted Hue to some sort of crisis, as she returned from taking little Helene to school. What now? She wondered. Hearing the uncontrolled barking of Monsieur's pack of dogs, a chill ran between her shoulder blades. She quickened the pace, reaching the garden entrance through the kitchen. Outside, she was met by a vociferous barrage of expletives. Cook was standing by the stacks of rice bags, arms whirling like a windmill, pointing repeatedly in the direction of the well. In front of her stood Monsieur's turbaned servant, impassive in the face of all the agitation. From behind him rose a direct path to a disused well that had once provided the house with drinking water, until Madame had insisted a civilised life required access to running water. Nowadays, the gardeners occasionally used the well as a back-up to water the plants furthest from the mains. Something bad had happened. Maybe one of the gardeners had fallen in, unable to climb up? No, this didn't account for the dogs, Hue thought. That's when she noticed the torn bags of rice littering the environs of Arthur's shed.

At the school gates a few hours later, Hue paced in short circles, a deep frown creasing her usually perfectly smooth complexion. What was she supposed to tell little Helene now?

As if on cue, the doors opened, releasing a swarm of primary school children in a buzz of excitement. Hue spotted Helene, her small legs carrying her forward in an erratic dance that contrasted with the idea of decorum Madame was so desperate to instil in her daughter. Her warm body collided with Hue's and the latter was forced to smile. "Good day in school?" she asked.

"Delightful," the girl replied, before taking the hand Hue offered and following her governess home, adopting the woman's more reserved cadence.

"I can't wait to see Arthur," Helene commented after a while. "Oh, Hue. Do you think he missed me?"

Hue's countenance wavered for a second. She tightened her grip around the little hand and pushed on without saying a word. Monsieur would want to tell the girl himself. Hue pressed her lips together. Her employer's manners were brusque and direct at the best of times. Her heart broke at the thought of the sweet child being confronted with what Monsieur would call 'the realities of life'. In the lobby, they found Madame waiting, back straight, her hands clasped together into a tight knot. "Your father wants a word with you, dear child. You will find him in his study."

Later that night, Hue helped a mute Helene to put on her nightdress. The girl hadn't spoken a word all evening. As she slid under the covers, Hue thought she heard a repressed sob. Taking hold of Helene's hand, she leant close to her ear and whispered, "Can I tell you a secret?"

Helene's eyes widened and she gave a tentative nod.

"Arthur is not really gone. You see, the garden was getting too small for him. He wanted to explore beyond the wall."

"But Father said ..."

Hue placed a finger against her lips. "Grown-ups are so serious they forget to see the world for what it is. A place of wonder."

"You mean ..."

"Arthur is a magical bear. Since you are such a good girl, as soon as you close your eyes and fall asleep, he will come visit you in your dreams. Maybe ... if you are really good, he will take you on one of his journeys."

"Where do you think he is now?"

"Let's see ..." Hue stood and walked to the desk, returning with a large, illustrated atlas. She opened it to a random page. "Give me your finger," she told Helene, inviting her to point anywhere on the map. "Here we are. Rabat. Your bear is in North Africa, a country called Morocco. If you're quick, you can meet him there," she added, closing the atlas with a big thud. Hue recounted to Helene the tale of how her pet bear had eaten so much rice that he had inflated into

17

a balloon, rising above the garden wall, and floating away. Every night after that, Helene rushed to bed without an argument, eager to fall asleep so that Arthur could come and collect her.

In the morning, she told Hue about how the girl and the bear had hopped from cloud to cloud in the night, describing in detail the marvels of each new country they had explored together.

Maman

My mother often shared fond memories of growing up in Rabat. Of her brother Jean. Their parents' house had a flat terrace, surrounded by a large and luxurious garden, filled with colourful fruits gorged with the sweetness of sunlight. There, she said, they played together with children from Christian, Jewish, and Muslim families. Everyone dressed in bright summer clothes, hid in bushes, absorbed in a perpetual game of hide-and-seek. She would tell of the time when she had climbed a tree after Jean, intent on stealing ripe fruits. She had fallen in the large vat of rainwater below, a container in which small dead birds were often found. The Moroccan gardener had fished her out of the foul water tank, while her mother, between hysterical screams, exhorted her not to behave like a savage, and her brother contributed to the chaos with loud fits of laughter. As she told it, my mother had been grounded for a week, whilst Jean had escaped unscathed, being the boy who could do no wrong.

As an adult, my mother had defied conventions, moving to the UK from Morocco aged eighteen, then travelling to South America, where she had lived for the best part of a decade, working as an air hostess on international long-haul flights. Of that period, she would mention the many countries she had visited, focusing on sensational snippets: the giant tarantula found in her shoe that first night in Australia; an elephant ride in a nameless Indian village where she had eaten the hottest of curries; restrictions on women bathers in Franco's Spain ... From those small vignettes that said very little about my mother's daily life, I had built the picture of an exotic adventurer, a woman traveller who feared neither danger nor the weight of convention.

Istanbul

The first journey I recorded into Uncle Jean's travel journal was a trip I took with my parents in the early nineties, to Istanbul. My mother had booked a room in the Pera Palace, once a stop on the mythical Orient Express journey. We were meant to spend five days visiting the city's landmarks: the Blue Mosque, Topkapi, Aya Sophia, and the Grand Bazaar.

When we landed and the air hostess opened the plane door, we were hit by a foul smell. The rubbish collectors for the city had been on strike for three weeks, and despite the cold weather (it was snowing), the stench was eye-watering. Our hotel room was on the second floor. We reached it through an ancient-looking lift, operated by a man in a red and gold outfit, a small rectangular hat perched on top of his head.

"Oh, I want a costume like that," I told my dad who squeezed my hand hard.

In the room, we found there was only a double bed.

"Where do I sleep?" I asked, feeling forgotten.

My mother called reception, then turned towards me, eyes locked onto my father's face.

"He said they thought we were travelling with a baby. They are sending someone now."

After a few minutes, we heard a rasping knock on the door. My mother sent me to open it and a small woman in a grey housekeeper outfit came through the door, eyes glued to the carpet.

"Bed," she said, walking towards a small couch, what the French would call a *banquette Second-Empire*. She drew a sheet across the hard surface, placed a pillow at one end and a blanket over the top, then retreated towards the door.

I opened my mouth to object, but my mother raised a hand, and I remained quiet.

"It is only for a few days," she told me once the woman had left. "Let's draw you a bath, then we can tuck you in."

As if on cue, my father removed his shoes and lay down, stretching the length of the bed, absorbed in the tourist guidebook he had brought along with him. "Did you know, the Pera Palace where we are staying is the hotel where the British author Agatha Christie wrote *Murder on the Orient Express*," he told my mother. "Isn't it one of your mother's favourite books?"

In the bathroom of white marble, two golden taps hung over the largest sink I had ever seen. Awesome, I thought. I went to turn one of the taps. It gurgled for a minute, then a yellow liquid filled the sink, and with it the smell of rotten eggs.

"What now?" my mother asked as I came running into their room.

"The water. There is something wrong with the water."

My father rose reluctantly, placing the guidebook upside-down on the bedside table. "Let's have a look," he said with a sigh, walking around the bed and into the bathroom.

"Let me show you," I told him, as if presenting an exhibit at the zoo.

"Right," he replied.

"What's that smell, Dad?"

"Sulphur. And the colour is rust. I guess nobody has used this bathroom for a while. Just run the water until it is clear and don't swallow when you brush your teeth."

His advice given, he left me standing there, eyeing the foul-smelling water with suspicion. After a minute, the sulphurous odour dissipated. A pool of water had formed on the inside of the sink, leaving a stained rim the colour of turmeric all around. Closing the tap, I ran back into the room, grabbed my cuddly bear, and jumped into the makeshift bed.

"Goodnight," my parents called from the bed, as if they occupied a neighbouring island.

Of Istanbul, I recorded the size of the emeralds at Topkapi castle, the nice pretzel-looking bread that vendors sold in the bazaar, and the large shields inside Ayasofya, once a church, now a mosque, a place transformed at the vagaries of successive occupiers.

On the last day, as we were waiting for a taxi to take us back to the airport, I saw a man selling roasted chestnuts on the other side of the road.

"We have those at home," I pointed. Then I noticed the chain and the bear tied to the man's cart. A customer approached them and handed a small glass bottle to the vendor. The latter yanked on the chain and the bear straightened, revealing a tap protruding from its stomach. Bringing the bottle closer, he unscrewed the top and poured a greenish liquid from the bear's stomach.

"Bile," my father explained, seeing my horrified face. "People drink it for health."

I looked whilst the bear collapsed back into a ball, the smell of roasted chestnuts filling my nostrils. I felt a strong urge to vomit, pressed my cuddly bear against my chest and repressed a sob.

"What really happened to Arthur?" I asked my mother.

"Who?"

"Arthur, Bonne-Maman's pet bear?"

"I'm not sure sweetheart. You'll have to ask her."

Fez

I recorded another trip in the journal. That one to Morocco, taken with my parents earlier, when I was maybe five or six. In my memory is a large courtyard tiled with blue and turquoise geometric patterns, a balcony leading to a series of wooden doors, one being the bedroom I shared with my parents, and an imposing woman, despite her short stature, dressed in a black *djellaba*, a line of faded indigo ink marking her wrinkled chin down the middle. I seem to recall that she not so much walked as she shuffled, her leather *babouches* sliding on the floor as if parting from the ground would cause her pain.

In my mind, her name is Fatima, and she is connected to my mother somehow. I remember feeling an immense sense of affection for this strange woman. I recall her taking me by the hand and walking out of the house into an empty street, past a mechanic's garage, to a little stand where she bought a bag of flour. It was early, and the morning light reverberated off the sand-coloured buildings lining the street, tinting the memory pink.

Back at the house, Fatima took me to the kitchen and taught me how to bake semolina bread for my parents. Once the *kesra* was cooked, she tore off a piece and offered it to me. My taste buds became possessed with a strange frenzy, the flavour titillating the tip of my tongue, so that I kept telling Fatima, "More, more, more."

Instead, she sent me to play in the courtyard, urging me to be quiet so as not to wake my parents. In my heart, the woman is an extension of family, maybe *la fatma* who once raised my mother and uncle. As I look back now, maybe she was simply the kind-hearted owner of the boarding house where we stayed. Memories can be deceiving.

A few days later, we visited Fez, crystallised years later in my travel journal as an afternoon in the Medina, drinking mint tea from small gold-chiselled glasses that a waiter expertly poured from a little silver teapot raised up high. Everything else I forgot.

Utah

The last entry in my journal is dated 1996 – a final trip with my parents, travelling the length of Utah to the National Parks – Lake Placid, Grand Canyon, stopping to visit Las Vegas. The trip lasted two weeks, which we spent mostly on the road, driving from one park to the next, roaming long stretches of empty roads, listening to local radio stations blaring rock classics that reminded my parents of their youth. Each night, we stopped at a Best Western hotel. Everywhere the same format. Everywhere the same food. All-you-can-eat buffets. Crackers. Stringy cheese and onion soup. Corrugated jugs of amber iced tea. Prawn cocktail salad with sweet Marie-Rose sauce.

Of this journey, I retain a single postcard, pressed between two blank pages of my travel journal: a blue sky framed by a red rock arch, memento of an excursion I took with my father to the Nevada Proving Grounds, sixty-five miles northwest of Las Vegas. A place where, in 1951, the US dropped nuclear bombs to test their effects. The ground oozed with green and pink foam, as if a child had coloured it in. At one point, we parked, and my father stepped out of the car to take pictures. Shortly after, a large GM pickup truck with 'private security' written in wide lettering on the side reached us. A uniformed man stepped out, with short-cropped hair and the demeanour of an army personnel. As he approached, I noticed the tension of his hand, hovering over a side arm. "Can I ask what you are doing here, sir?" he asked my father, putting a heavy emphasis on the 'sir'. Seemingly unfazed, my father replied that we were French tourists holidaying along the National Parks, that we had lost our way and would welcome his assistance. Hearing this, the armed man eyed the rental sticker on our car, motioned for me to lower the window, and addressed me directly, creaking his neck so he could make eye contact. "Is your father nice?" he asked, a peculiar question heavy with meaning. I nodded yes, which seemed to satisfy his professional suspicion. Releasing the tension in his hand, he directed my father to approach. "This is a restricted area, sir," he explained, in a gentler voice. "You can't be here." He gestured in my direction.

"Apologies," my father replied. "I lost my bearings."

The security guard took another look at me and invited my father to re-enter the vehicle. "Follow me," he said. "I'll return you to the main road."

In the car, I stared at my father as he drove at pace, following the man in his enormous van. "Were we really lost?" I asked once the guard had waved us off.

He placed one finger against his lips. "Sometimes it is better to let people believe you are lost," he said, smiling.

2. ASSIMILATION

Bouknadel

Marianne had woken early in her parents' house in Rabat, excited by the prospect of this special day. It was 1961 and Marcel Francis, an eccentric French horticultural engineer with a passion for Morocco, was due to reveal to the public his life's work, an ambitious park developed on a bare plot of land he had purchased in the 1950s on the Rabat to Kenitra road. In ten years, he had transformed four and a half hectares of disused land into a celebration of natural beauty and horticulture, a garden of grandiose proportions spread alongside the Atlantic coastline, offering the visitor a multitude of paths, inspired by cultures from around the world. Visitors were invited to meander amongst a diverse and luxurious vegetation which he wished to preserve for future generations. The grand opening was the talk of Rabat, and everyone would be at the lunch reception.

Marianne rode the twelve kilometres from Rabat to Bouknadel on her bicycle. As she entered the garden, she was mesmerised by the delicate water features interspersed along the path. She paused to read discreet information boards scattered along the flower beds, offering details about the provenance and particularities of the colourful plants that had been harmonised into an idyllic haven for all to enjoy.

As she reached her group of friends, Marianne spotted her older cousin, on a visit for the holiday.

"Elizabeth. How are you?" Elizabeth was a nurse married to a senior intelligence officer from Paris. She was the picture of what Marianne's mother considered a respectable woman.

Elizabeth kissed her on both cheeks. "Marianne, finally. You found us. Isn't this place wonderfully exotic?"

"It is. I love the water fountains," she replied.

"The boys have improvised a game of football. Everyone is here."

"And what about this one," Marianne asked, pointing at a tall boy seemingly undisturbed by the strain of the game, "Who is he?"

"Francis. I brought him along. Our mothers are friends," Elizabeth explained.

"I don't think I've ever met him," Marianne replied.

"Oh, he goes to boarding school on the mainland," Elizabeth added. "His family lives in Rabat. He is visiting for the summer."

After the game, they headed to the celebration. Local men of importance made innocuous speeches. Wives cut ribbons.

"Here you are, Sis," Jean called, spinning Marianne around and giving her a twirl. "I don't suppose you saw Rashid in all that vegetation?" he asked.

"Rashid, the gardener? What do you want him for?"

"Never mind that. Shall we?" He gave a mock bow, before offering Marianne his arm.

Tables had been spread for Rabat's finest on the main lawn. Everyone was eager to be seen and savour a free lunch. The parents, dressed for the occasion, intimated their disappointment at the regrettable nonchalance of their offspring. Oblivious, the youth sought their own sources of entertainment, making acerbic remarks about Madame Marcel's straw hat, and gabbling about the fact her husband already seemed to have had one too many. Taking advantage of Marianne's fits of giggles, Elizabeth sat the new boy next to her cousin, making certain to sit opposite to observe the show. The laughter had died down by the time Marianne noticed Francis next to her. Used to boys being self-assured and exuberant, she found his quiet demeanour intriguing. Mistaking his silence for shyness at first, she soon noticed the way he kept himself aback, watching everyone around him. Their eyes crossed and Marianne swiftly feigned disinterest, reaching across the table to quiz her cousin about life as an officer's wife in Paris. Marianne was envious. At eighteen, she had never been anywhere. Soon, her brother Jean, who had recently completed journalism studies, would be leaving to pursue a career as a reporter. Their stepfather had secured a post for him through a fellow officer he had treated on the front, during the Second World War. As time went on, it felt like everyone in her generation was leaving. She feared being left behind, one of those old spinsters caring for their ageing parents.

The feeling of being watched interrupted her train of thought.

"Impressive garden party," Francis commented as if talking to himself.

"There is very little else to do around here," she conceded, with a smile. "Don't let today fool you. Normally we are all routine. Lunch at the club, beach in the afternoon, church on Sunday, that kind of thing," she added. "This is the most excitement we have had in weeks, in fact. Everyone who matters is here." As she said it, Marianne made a grand gesture with her arm, as if introducing the boy to the crowd assembled.

"I don't know anyone. I only met Elizabeth this morning actually," he replied, half apologetic. "Her husband was one of my tutors at the academy."

She presented him with her hand to shake – "Marianne, how do you do?"

"Charmed," he replied, bowing his head – "Francis."

"I know," she replied with a pinched laugh. "You're news, you see."

He raised a quizzical eyebrow.

Ignoring his reaction, she continued. "Will you be joining us later, to the beach I mean?"

He seemed to consider the question, his slate-coloured eyes taking in the symmetry of her face. As he did, she could feel a little vein pulsating at the base of her neck.

"I would like that very much," he said – and after a pause – "spending more time getting to know you, I mean."

Fez

The next morning, the phone rang. It was Elizabeth. Francis was asking whether Marianne would join them on a day trip to Fez. Not so shy then, Marianne thought.

"Jean, are you coming? We are going to Fez with Elizabeth."

"I'm alright, thanks little sis. Why don't you invite your new boyfriend?" Marianne stuck out her tongue. Nothing escaped her brother. "I saw the two of you getting comfortable yesterday," he grinned. That was it. He was going to tease her relentlessly. She couldn't wait for him to get a girlfriend so she could return the favour.

A few minutes later, Elizabeth parked outside Marianne's house, Francis jumped out and knocked on the door. "Your chariot awaits," he bellowed, bowing, as she opened the door and stepped past him.

In the Medina, they marvelled at the architectural beauty of the place with its whitewashed terraced cafés offering mint tea served in small hand-painted glasses, accompanied by crescent-shaped almond pastries.

After lunch, Elizabeth proposed to show them the open-sky Chouara tannery. It was one of the biggest of its kind, she explained.

The gate opened on a vast courtyard filled with large stone vessels, sealed to one another by a narrow ledge, giving the impression a giant painter had rested his palette there for a moment.

"Each vessel is filled with multicoloured dyes made out of poppy, indigo, or henna," Elizabeth explained.

"What's that smell?" Marianne asked, the content of her stomach rising in her throat.

"Oh, that. The tanners mix the dye with cow urine, salt, water, and pigeon faeces to fix the colour to the leather."

"That's disgusting."

"The *babouches* you buy from the souk come from here," Francis pointed out, an amused look on his face. "Anyone brave enough to walk across?"

Marianne wasn't prepared to be defeated. "Of course," she replied, defiant, grabbing Elizabeth by the arm and dragging her along with her.

It was hot as the three of them started their progression, single file, behind a little wiry man, one of the tanners, fast and sure-footed. The path meandered along a ledge only as wide as the foot, delineating a multitude of pools of colours. Marianne tried not to look down, concentrating instead on the distance to cover before she would be back on firm ground. The smell of death emanating from the vats was overwhelming around her, the afternoon heat distorting the air. Nauseated, she repressed the urge to run off, driven to impress Francis. The next moment, her foot slipped. Everything happened in slow motion. She emitted a sound that was more whimper than scream, horrified at the idea she was about to drown in foul toxins. As she closed her eyes, she felt a force lifting her body up, holding on to her tight, and depositing her back onto firm ground. When she reopened her eyes, Elizabeth was staring at her, a mocking expression on her face. Looking up, she saw Francis, his concerned face framed by blond, almost white, hair. "Are you alright?" he asked. He looked angelic, she thought. Speechless, maybe for the first time in her life, Marianne simply nodded in response.

"It is just the smell," he added, his forehead relaxing.

"Maybe we should head back?" Elizabeth interjected.

All the way home, Francis kept a watchful eye through the rear-view mirror, as if Marianne might fall off the vehicle at any moment.

"What's with him?" Marianne asked her cousin, later that night.

"The boy has a hero complex if you ask me. His father was a decorated officer who fell in combat before Francis was born. It is a hard act to follow for a boy. His mother had him sent to military academy in the Sartre."

"Where is that?"

"Mainland France. Somewhere in the middle. Apparently, she

dropped him off there when he was six and told him to make his father proud."

"How do you know that?"

"His father served with Armand."

"Your husband and his father?"

"Yes. The two families are close. Armand kept an eye on him when he was doing his military service. According to him, he is very promising."

Marianne marvelled at this intriguing boy who told stories of visits to Alger, West and East Berlin and was due to start his studies in Paris in the autumn. His life certainly beat the tedium of Rabat where men conducted business at the club whilst their wives kept the help in check and meddled in everyone's private life. Marianne imagined how delightful it would be to live a life not regimented by gossip.

Rabat

The summer was coming to an end.

"Take me with you," Marianne begged, eyes filling with tears.

Francis looked at her, uncertain. "This has been the best holiday I have ever had, but I have my studies to consider. I can't afford any distraction."

Her tears redoubled then. She threw herself to the ground. Told him she could do the cleaning and the cooking whilst he studied. He remained unresponsive, visibly uncomprehending.

"I beg you."

"We have only known each other for four weeks," he replied, painfully reasonable.

She was wailing now, rolling on the floor like a child in the fit of a tantrum.

"What brought this on?" he asked.

She shook her head. Her cries suddenly muted.

"I'm so sorry."

Marianne turned swollen eyes towards the window, repressing another sob.

"Goodbye Marianne," Francis uttered as he exited the room.

Jean

That morning, Marianne barged into Jean's bedroom, bouncing on the bed as he hid under the covers.

"You're awake?" she shrieked.

"Leave me alone."

"There is a garden party at the club. Everyone is going to be there. Mum said I could go if you go."

"Fat chance. I'm meeting a friend. Ask Elizabeth to chaperone you." Marianne pouted at her brother. "Pleeeeeaaase!"

"Alright, then. Just for a bit."

She launched to kiss him on the cheek. "You're the best."

Jean remembered the affection he felt for this exuberant little sister of his as she tornadoed her way out of the room. He rolled out of bed and headed for the bathroom where he shaved, took a shower, and applied a liberal amount of aftershave. The whole town would be at the club today. Ideal, he thought. He checked his naked reflection in the mirror.

"Hello handsome," he called out loud to the tanned, muscular reflection staring back at him. He thought about Rashid. The thought made him smile.

It had happened without either of them noticing. There had been exchanged looks. Something passing between them. A signal, subtle enough to be deniable. A connection growing with every sustained second. Then one day, Jean's hand had inadvertently brushed against Rashid's naked arm as they were passing in the garden. Instead of pulling away, Rashid had turned and grabbed Jean's forearm, pulling him close. They had remained there for a minute, taking the measure of one another. It was Jean who had pulled away first.

"Not here," he had said, looking around to check whether they had been seen.

"Where?" Rashid had replied with urgency.

"The dunes. This afternoon." The dunes beyond the car park,

through the wooded area, and into the relative anonymity of acres of sand mounds and deep wadis, where men like him met with other men. And so, their relationship had grown, in secret. In company, Jean had continued to act with the expected degree of indifference, hiding what everyone else would have seen as a shameful entanglement.

After the club, Jean travelled to the beach car park. Relieved to find it deserted, he called Rashid's name in the wind, heading towards their usual meeting point. As he went, he watched the mounds of sand, held together by a carpet of creeping sour figs, their green claws rising from the ground like messengers of doom. The crunching of sand coming from behind startled him. Before he could turn, a heavy body had forced him to the ground. A familiar earthy scent. Turning, promptly, he registered the line of Rashid's jaw, soothed by his contagious smile.

"Hello, *habibi*," Jean said, sealing the words with a kiss. The men rolled into a natural recess between two banks, entwined, part-wrestlers, part-lovers, peeling clothes off as they went. There they stayed, baked by the sun, oblivious to a world where their love had no place. Elsewhere, maybe. But not in Rabat. Not then. Jean had promised Rashid he would take him away. Elsewhere. Soon.

Three years Jean's junior, Rashid often reminded him he had more to lose if they got caught. Of course, the law would hold Jean responsible since he had just reached the age of sexual consent, but for Rashid the danger lay in appearances. People here would never accept what their relationship implied. Jean dismissed those fears, drunk with love and the freedom his career as a journalist would soon provide.

"Did you hear something?"

Jean stretched his neck, bringing his ear closer to the invisible sound. "It is the wind *habibi*, there is no one here." Reassured, Rashid buried his face in Jean's warm neck. When they heard the scream, it was too late. Elizabeth was standing on the ridge of the dune, overlooking their nakedness. She ran, shrieking. They followed, slowed by the sand collapsing under their feet, shaken in shame and the urgency to cover their bodies, to hide, to run their separate ways. They waved, shouted. It wasn't what she thought.

At home, the police were already waiting. It was Elizabeth who had called them. She was standing in the middle of the living room, flanked by Jean's mother. Righteous.

"How could you?" Elizabeth yelled. Jean stuttered, tried to explain, the sound of his own beating heart deafening. Just then, he noticed Rashid, framed by two officers.

"What are you doing? Rashid hasn't done anything wrong," he screamed, his voice coming out like a plea.

"You don't understand the realities of life," his mother replied. "Officer, tell him."

"Son, you will be charged with statutory rape. The boy is three years your junior."

Instead of executing his ominous warning, the policeman seemed to hesitate. An imperceptible nod passed between him and Jean's mother.

"You can't let them take me away, Mother," Jean cried. "We didn't do anything!"

She straightened as she turned her back away from her son to face the uniformed man. "Officer," she said, in a conciliatory tone. "Clearly this Rashid is to blame for leading my son astray. Something must be done, surely."

"Yes, Ma'am." The officer replied, all too eager. He gestured and his men pulled on Rashid's arm, forcing his limp body to jerk forward.

"Would you mind using the back door, officer? The neighbours ..."

"Of course, Ma'am."

Jean watched motionless as the officers dragged his lover off, through the garden to a door which he knew led to a back alley. From there, the sound of heavy thuds and muffled screams shook the silence.

"Rashid," Jean murmured.

"Stop this nonsense," his mother pronounced, her jaw clamped shut. "What were you thinking? Get out of my sight."

That's when Jean caught a heavy sob and noticed Marianne for the first time. Her eyes were swollen with tears. He went to reach her, but she stepped back. Outside, the sound of Rashid's cries had stopped. Jean fell to his knees, arms reaching forward as if grasping after a ghost. Marianne stepped out of the shadow then and grabbed hold of his arm. She tried to help him up, noticed the erratic jolting of his eyes between their mother and the door.

"Leave him," their mother said.

London

The Dubois were a French family from Paris. They resided in a rented terraced house on Pimlico Road. Marc, the husband, worked at the French Embassy. Madame Dubois – Marie-Louise – was from an old French family, and it was evidently her connections that had landed her husband this diplomatic post, rather than any natural ability on his part. As soon as they had arrived, Madame Dubois had saddled herself with the task of securing a full-time nanny for the children. An acquaintance at the Alliance Française had recommended an eighteen-year-old girl from a good family, fresh from Rabat.

"You are part of the family, of course," Madame Dubois told Marianne at their first meeting. "Monsieur Dubois and I are very busy with our social commitments. It will fall upon you to ensure the children retain good French values. You understand of course."

Marianne was not certain she did understand, nonetheless, she nodded politely.

Tim and Elsa were small, six and four respectively. Marianne's role was to dress them, feed them, entertain them, ensure they walked to the park twice daily and went to bed at a suitable time. All those tasks were codified on the schedule Madame Dubois had handed Marianne on her first day.

Bedtime was Marianne's favourite with the children. After their bath, she would tuck them into bed and regale them with stories of adventures set in magical gardens inspired from her own childhood. She described the pink bougainvillea, white laurel trees and blue clematis with vivid details.

"At night," she told them, "The air is filled with the heavy scent of jasmine. The plant we call the night watchman." In Tim and Elsa's heads, she planted green giants crowned with delicate white flowers, wielding large scimitars to slay turbaned djinns intent on stealing children's dreams. For Tim's birthday, she painted a picture of a mysterious desert creature, half-dog, half-fox, the colour of dunes, and ears as big as bats. "It can track your steps from miles away," she told him. "We call it a fennec." Tim took the small painting of the little desert fox and disappeared into his bedroom with his treasure, under the disapproving gaze of Madame Dubois.

Six days a week, Marianne cared for the children from dusk till dawn. On her one day off, she took the bus to Harrods on Brompton Road for high tea. In this temple of luxury, Marianne sat, ordered a pot of tea, and observed the international clientele. Women wrapped in rivers of pearls, fur coats, and the distinct scent of money. On one of those days, Marianne spotted Madame Dubois at one of the tables, in conversation with an elegant woman. She could tell from the intonations that carried that they were speaking French. Since it was her day off, she thought she would join them.

"Mesdames," she said, pulling up a chair.

"Finally," the elegant woman said, hardly gracing her with a glimpse. "A pot of Earl Grey, please."

Marianne turned to Madame Dubois with a dry little cough, waiting for her to clear the misunderstanding. At first, she averted her eyes.

"Marie-Louise?" Marianne insisted.

Forced to acknowledge her employee, Madame Dubois emitted a small laugh. "It's you Marianne. I hadn't recognised you standing there. What in heavens are you doing in Harrods?" Without waiting for Marianne to respond, she turned to her friend, "Geneviève, this is our new nanny, Marianne. A real pearl."

"*Enchantée*. And where are you from?"

"Rabat," Marianne replied.

"I see." The woman's eyebrow raised imperceptibly. "And how are you finding London dear? It must seem so ... civilised."

It was less a question than a statement. Marianne stood for a few more seconds, still holding the back of the chair.

"I'll see you at home then," Madame Dubois finally said,

punctuating her words with a wave of the hand. Before Marianne had let go of the chair, the two women had resumed their conversation.

As she walked away, it dawned on Marianne that those women with their large hats and perfectly manicured hands considered themselves to be a different society, one that tiptoed on impossibly high heels whilst girls like her crawled on all fours to care for their children. The next morning, Marianne was building a castle out of blankets and pillows in the living room for Tim and Elsa when Madame Dubois walked in.

"Children, can you go to your room please. Marianne and I have some details to discuss."

Reluctantly, the children rose from their kingdom of soft cushions and made their way upstairs. Madame Dubois stood, framed by the light from the corridor, watching whilst Marianne hurried to tidy the living room. When she was done, Madame Dubois took a deep inhale and spoke in slow, detached words. "Monsieur Dubois and I have spoken. We agree. This ..." she gestured towards where the castle had stood a moment before, "... is not a good fit. The children, they need discipline. A firm hand. You ... fill their heads with nonsense."

Marianne went to open her mouth, but no sound came out.

"Understand," Madame Dubois continued. "We realise it isn't your fault. They obviously don't do things the same way overseas. We ... we thought we would have a similar vision of things, you see."

No, Marianne didn't see.

"We don't want to make it hard on the children, though. It is best if you go and pack your bags now."

Marianne stared at her heavy black leather shoes as her feet carried her up the stairs to the little room adjacent to the children's bedroom. She felt dislocated, as if the shoes belonged to someone else. She pulled her small suitcase from under the bed, opened it and stacked her belongings inside. Clothes. Pictures. A portable watercolour set. She moved like an automaton. As she dragged the suitcase downstairs, she noticed the muffled sound of Tim and Elsa growing fainter. At the front door, Madame Dubois was waiting, a sealed envelope in one hand. "Your payment to the end of the week, and a letter of reference," she said, drily. Marianne stepped outside and Madame Dubois closed the door behind her.

Paris

Wilson had been born the eldest of twelve siblings in a small Yoruba village in western Nigeria. Following in his father's footsteps, he was fated to become the next village doctor. A bright pupil, all hopes had been placed on him. The neighbours had clubbed together to buy him passage to the United States to attend medical school. It was the wish of the elders that Wilson train there, then return to the village to take over from his father. The university fees had been covered. The plane ticket that would take him to New York via Charles de Gaulle had been purchased, the transfer fee paid.

Maybe the agent who arranged the trip had been less than scrupulous, or maybe along the administrative trail of paperwork spanning three countries, a document had not been stamped in the right place. Either way, when Wilson presented himself to the transfer desk in Paris, he was asked to accompany a uniformed man to an office cubicle painted magnolia. Once seated, the agent requested he give up his Nigerian passport and presented him with a stack of coloured papers. For hours, he filled forms in triplicate. Pink sheet, blue sheet, green sheet. The white copy was for him to keep, the uniform said. Wilson approached the delay with the patience of a man used to cumbersome administrative meandering. He had a ticket, he reminded himself. The plane to New York would not be leaving without him. The uniformed man took him to a grey waiting area with orange plastic chairs bolted to the linoleum floor and invited him to sit a second time, without as much as a smile. Four other men were already in the room. Claver and Patrice from Rwanda greeted Wilson in Kinyarwanda. Wilson smiled an apologetic smile. "I am Mamadou, from Cameroon," a jovial looking man in his thirties added, stretching out his hand for Wilson to shake. The fourth was dressed in an impeccably tailored suit, the likes of which Wilson had only seen in Abuja Central District, Maitama and Garki. Seated a little to one side, the man didn't introduce himself, checking his watch twice in the time it took for Wilson to settle.

"Ṣe o tí n dúró pẹ?" Wilson asked him.

"Seventeen hours," the businessman replied in English. "They made me miss my flight."

On hearing this, Wilson frowned. "Surely, they have to put you on the next flight?"

"We are all the same to them," the businessman replied, waving at the other men.

"But I am only in transit here," Wilson protested.

The businessman shrugged and returned to his observation of the slow passing of time.

Hours went by. Mamadou rolled his sweatshirt into a ball, placed it under his head, and lay the length of three plastic chairs. He fell asleep in minutes.

The next morning, a different uniformed man came in to inform the five men that they would have to attend a meeting a day later, when their immigration status would be determined. In the meantime, the officer added, their passports would be held back. He handed them a leaflet written in a dozen languages, giving details of a temporary shelter for new arrivals. Someone would be expecting them. Wilson tried to protest, but the uniformed man was unmoved. Mamadou patted him on the shoulder. "Come," he told him in accented English. Stunned by the border officer's indifference, Wilson followed Mamadou, Claver, and Patrice as they left the airport, and made their way towards a bus stop, talking the whole time in such rapid-fire French that each word seemed to merge into the next. It occurred to Wilson that he was shipwrecked in a city he knew nothing about. Better follow Mamadou and the others who seemed to know where they were heading.

Only the one night, Wilson told himself when he saw the queues of bedraggled families outside the shelter. The tired-looking woman at reception gave him a pile of leaflets and encouraged Wilson to sign up for French classes the next day, commenting that the French administration had no patience for those unwilling to assimilate.

Wilson argued that he had no intention of remaining in France, repeating the word 'traveller' over and over again. The woman waved her hand in a universal gesture of dismissal and moved on to the next person in the line. The misadventure would soon be cleared up, and he could continue his journey to New York, he reassured himself. It would become one of those family anecdotes his mother fed to the neighbours.

Except the simple misadventure soon turned into a significant delay.

"Sorry, sir," the woman behind the ticket counter told him when he handed her his passport. "Your transit visa has expired."

At the US Embassy, he was told that there was a considerable waiting time for tourist visa appointments during the summer months. "Maybe you ought to return to Nigeria," the Embassy employee suggested.

"You don't understand," Wilson exploded. "I'm due to start medical school in a few weeks. See, I have a student visa." He tapped on the colourful square glued to the page of his passport.

"This is not valid here, sir," the woman said, detaching every word. "It says here your visa is to travel from Nigeria. You will have to return to Nigeria and travel from there."

Wilson placed his head in his hands. It had taken months for his family to come up with the price of the original ticket. By the time they sent him money for two new tickets he would have missed the start of term in New York. The judge had granted him temporary stay. Two months was tight, but maybe he could purchase the tickets himself if he could only find a job.

Back at the shelter, he climbed the narrow stairs to his single room, a box with bars on the window, overlooking a blind concrete wall, decorated with a poster advertising *Back to the Future*'s cinema release. Moving to the bed, he opened his suitcase and sighed at the contents. He had planned for university life, bringing jeans, t-shirts, and casual shirts. He would need to ask the lady at reception for a jacket and tie from the donated pile she had pointed out to him on arrival. Dropping onto the mattress, Wilson released a cloud of dust from the bed cover into the air and sneezed. Closing his eyes, he imagined his mother's warm hand on his back, a concerned frown searching for signs of discomfort. She was a formidable woman, his mother. She had given birth to fourteen children. Their games breathed life into the compound that doubled as a surgery from which Wilson's father had cared for whole communities since the 1960s. In the courtyard, the children ran after the chickens that some patients brought as payment, weaving around groups of mothers and the sick children they carried from miles away to the only local doctor. They would crouch in a circle, rocking the smallest children wrapped against their back, whilst erupting in Yoruba as they shared gossip from their village, where all the chores would be awaiting their return. It was because of these women that Wilson had elected to specialise in paediatrics.

At home, his own mother would be preparing food for his brothers and sisters, the smell of spiced grilled fish and boiled rice filling the air, whilst the kitchen echoed with joyful laughter as everyone gathered for the meal. All he had ever wanted was to make his mother proud. If she could see him now, he thought, surrounded by beggars...

Scanning the room for distractions, Wilson observed the way the floor bulged into a bubble at the foot of the bed, noticed the fan of bright leaflets scattered onto the linoleum. They had fallen off the bed when he sat down. For a moment, he brushed at them with his bare toes, looking at the unintelligible words against colourful backgrounds. It was no use, he thought, leaning forward to pick them up. His French was non-existent. But then his eye caught a familiar word: *étudiant*. Student. He couldn't understand the rest, but the illustration showed smiling boys and girls, rosy-cheeked and dressed in vivid t-shirts. Children – it felt like a sign. Turning the leaflet over, he found an address. That was it, he thought.

The next day, at the shelter, he waved the leaflet at the tired woman behind the counter. She picked it up and inspected it for a moment. *A oui, une agence de placement*, she nodded. Placements. Wilson had done office placements in Lagos thanks to his dad's connections, working on bespoke projects and being paid cash-in-hand. That would do just fine, he thought. He mimed straightening a tie, and the woman disappeared for a moment, returning with a blue blazer, white shirt, and orange tie. He pointed at his trouser legs, she responded with lifted shoulders, her hands upturned as if in hope of divine intervention. The jeans would have to do. As he headed out, she handed him two pieces of yellow cardboard with a brown strip in the middle, a map of the Paris underground, and a phonecard. *Metro*, she said. *Trocadero*.

Despite his linguistic handicap, Wilson found his way around the public transport system. He was used to large cities. Lagos had three times the population of the French capital. Immersing himself in the mass of tourists on the underground, he arrived at the Trocadero station, twenty minutes later, suddenly submerged by a flow of foreign languages that carried him, onto an esplanade overlooking the Eiffel Tower.

As he scanned the crowd, it seemed to Wilson that every nationality had come together in this place, united in the act of capturing a picture of Paris's famous landmark. On closer inspection, most of the tourists were white, or Japanese. Come to think of it, the only Black men on the esplanade were street vendors selling trinkets for the tourists, fluorescent glow sticks, small metal replicas of the Eiffel Tower, and wind-up pigeons, spread on a blanket on the ground, all stickered 'Made in Taiwan'. At one point, one of the men emitted a strident whistling sound, and all the men gathered the merchandise into their blanket, throwing the bundles over their shoulders as they ran for the safety of the park below, weaving amongst clusters of tourists. Less than a minute later, two uniformed police officers separated from the crowd, brushing past Wilson as they gave pursuit.

Following them as they disappeared amongst the trees, Wilson noticed loud music coming from beyond the balustrade. It came from a boombox balanced on the shoulder of a tall Black man on roller skates. The skater was gliding up the hill, placing little fluorescent cones along the red tarmacked path, like airport markers lighting the way to a wooden ramp, ready for take-off. When the skater reached the top of the hill, he placed the boombox onto the floor, and waited for a crowd to form. A handful of other skaters dressed in tight Adidas shorts and fluorescent leggings started to gather, moving to the sound of 1986's disco. After a while, tourists joined them, attracted by the promise of free entertainment. The skater started to clap his hands together high above his head in drawn-out motions, in tune with the music. Within a minute, the population of tourists on the esplanade had joined him in a strange universal anthem. The skater turned to his track then, and launched himself down the hill, zigzagging with measured effort, gathering speed, balancing his elbows to increase momentum, until he reached the ramp and, with an upward motion, propelled himself into the air, spreading his limbs far and wide, touching the tip of his skates with each hand, before collecting himself again, and landing without as much as a thud onto the ground, executing a semi-crescent to face the crowd, and finishing with a bow. The esplanade exploded with cheers, and joyful whistles, cameras clickety-clacking as apertures closed and opened, preserving the skater's prowess for posterity.

Elated, Wilson marched on in the direction of his appointment. At the door of the *agence*, he hesitated. He had expected an office block, rather than the little shop window that stood in front of him, reminding him of travel agencies lining Allen Avenue in Lagos. As he pushed the glass door open, a crystalline bell rang, announcing his presence. A grey-haired woman in a flowery dress with padded shoulders ill-suited to her pale complexion turned to greet him in a torrent of French words, none of which he understood.

"Sorry," he said, his word overlapping with hers, his feet retreating towards the door.

"Welcome," she spoke in English, moving towards him to offer him her hand. The word felt soothing. "Are you looking for a babysitter for your children?" she added.

Wilson blinked at the question, then thought to take the leaflet out of his pocket and handed it to the woman.

"I see," she said, lifting the winged glasses hanging around her neck to take a closer look. "Do you have any experience with children?"

Still unsure what she was talking about, Wilson nodded. "Twelve siblings," he said. "I am the eldest."

"Impressive," she replied. "And what brings you to Paris?"

Wilson thought before answering. When he did, he told the woman he was a medical student on his way to starting a degree in an American university and was spending a few weeks in Paris before term began. He was looking for a temporary arrangement, he added.

"Medical school. Excellent," she said, directing him to a chair.

She sat at a desk opposite, handing him a clipboard and a pen. He shrugged, in the manner French people seemed to favour.

"*Mon Français, ce n'ai pas bien,*" he added, apologetic.

"Right," she said. "I might have just the thing."

The woman pulled her chair around and sat with Wilson, translating the sections on the form, writing answers down on his behalf. Once she was done, she picked up the phone and spoke to someone in French, so fast that Wilson was unable to distinguish any space between the sounds. As she put the phone down, she smiled.

"It is as I thought," she said. "One of my clients is looking for an English-speaking student to babysit her daughter. Only child, the father works for the government and the mother is a painter. They travel a lot and the mother wants the child to be raised bilingually. She doesn't mind that you are ..." she waved at Wilson's full appearance. "You know ... a man."

Babysitting was not what Wilson had had in mind, but the exchange had made him realise that without a basic knowledge of

French, his work prospects would be limited. A child, he could manage, he thought.

"Thank you," he told the woman, shaking her hand in agreement. She gave him the address and instructed him to present himself the following morning. He decided to walk back to the shelter, thanking his ancestors for looking out for him.

Crossing a bridge over the river Seine, he noticed a small statue that reminded him of pictures of the Statue of Liberty. A bilingual sign informed him this was a miniature replica, a present from the people of the United States in exchange for the full-sized Lady Liberty paid for by the French, her benevolent gaze turned towards the huddled masses that populated that nation of migrants. To Wilson, this read like a good omen. In six weeks, he would be catching a flight, in time to start term in the Big Apple as planned. Stopping at a phone booth, he pulled out the phonecard and dialled the international code for Nigeria. It was good to hear the familiar warmth of his mother's voice. Yes, he had had a quiet journey and was settling into his hall of residence. Yes, the room was comfortable, but he missed her cooking already. Would he send a postcard of the Statue of Liberty, she asked? He thought for a moment, then promised.

Wilson tapped the backlit numbers on the golden keypad and entered the four-digit code. The little green LED flashed twice, and the imposing cast-iron door clicked. He pushed his shoulder against the pane to release the mechanism and stepped into a cold corridor leading to a second door, glass-panelled, and locked also. Either side of him, the walls were mounted with floor-to-ceiling mirrors. He noticed they created the illusion of an infinite number of reflections of himself, slowly growing smaller, until they became invisible to the naked eye. The vertiginous effect made him lose his bearings and he stumbled, catching himself onto the intercom that guarded the second door. Forcing himself to focus on the initials dancing in front of his eyes, he found the combination of letters he was looking for and pressed the button down in earnest, then waited. From above, the sound of running footsteps broke the silence.

"Allo?" A voice came out of the machine.

"Ça Wil-son," he articulated, as clearly as he could.

"Come in," the distorted voice replied in English. "First floor." And with that, a high-pitch buzz resonated from the lock, followed by another click.

Inside, a large staircase ran up, its wooden steps cushioned in thick carpet and held in place with brass clasps. The rich wool swallowed his footsteps, so that when the door of the apartment opened, the noise startled him. The lintel framed a short, middle-aged woman with ebony hair and a deep golden complexion, her slender frame wrapped in a vibrant kimono-style jacket with a large toucan head printed amongst exotic flowers.

Wilson had never seen a white woman wear such a bright outfit. She wore the colours of home, he thought. Instantly, he decided he would like her.

"I'm Marianne, do come in," she said in English, gesturing him in. They stepped into an opulent living room furnished with a mismatch of trinkets. "Family heirlooms," she explained, seeing Wilson eyeing each object with curiosity. She offered him coffee, scanning his face with the insistence of a painter, waiting for a sign he felt a little settled. After a long silence, she proceeded in flawless English. She was looking for a sitter for her eight-year-old daughter. The job would involve collecting her from primary school every day and taking her to the park. "Soon, it will be the summer holiday," she added. Then she would need round-the-clock support, whilst Marianne attended art classes. "I'm at the Beaux-Arts. Landscape painting," she explained.

Wilson nodded, unsure whether he was meant to react to the statement.

"The agency said you had experience with children?"

"Twelve siblings," he replied with a wide grin.

She met the answer with a smile of her own. "The agency said you are from Nigeria? Whereabouts?"

"The west of the country," Wilson replied, doubting this woman would be familiar with Nigerian geography.

"Near Ilorin?" she asked.

That startled Wilson. He took a fresh look at the woman. "Further north, a village near the Plateau," he clarified, his eyebrows raised in questioning.

"I was born in Morocco. Rabat. I followed my stepfather on his many trips across the continent. He was a doctor who dreamt to transform medical standards wherever he went," she added.

"My father is a doctor also," he replied, feeling more relaxed now. "A proud and patriotic man who shares similar dreams for our village."

"We are almost family then?" She exclaimed. "Your father must have passed on a strong sense of service to his son for you to agree to study medicine and return to your village. Your life won't be easy." She thought for a moment. "That settles it. It will be fifty francs per hour, meals included. And you can have the room upstairs, if you need."

Wilson did a quick mental calculation. If he worked throughout the summer, he would have enough for the two plane tickets, one back to Nigeria to get the correct visa, and one to New York, by the end of August. Enough time not to miss the start of term.

They shook hands. "I can teach you some French too, if you want," she added, still holding his hand in hers. "*They* don't take kindly to those who don't learn the language."

Wilson wondered who 'they' might be. Marianne explained that she had worked as an air hostess before she was married. She spoke five languages: French, English, Spanish, Italian, and Arabic.

Also working at the house was an elderly Spanish housekeeper who went by the name of Conchita. The teapot of a woman came four days a week to clean, iron, and prepare meals. The way the two exchanged rapid fire in Castilian reminded Wilson more of the back and forth in his mother's kitchen than what he would have expected from an employer–employee relationship in a Parisian apartment. He guessed that Conchita disapproved of his appointment, since she darted him sideways glances whenever she thought he wasn't looking. Marianne eventually swatted the air with one hand, and turned back to Wilson, handing him a large iron key tied to a yellow polka-dot ribbon. "Your room is that way," she pointed beyond Conchita at a reinforced door concealed between two dressers. "There is a separate staircase through the service entrance," she added.

Their business concluded, she invited him to get settled and return in the morning to meet his charge.

Back at the shelter, he packed his suitcase, thanked the receptionist for the shirt and jacket, and said goodbye with a sense of triumph. Only three days had passed since the lady had checked him in.

The room was on the top floor of the Haussmanien apartment building, one in a row of what he would learn had once been the servants' quarters, but now housed mostly students and a handful of Portuguese and Filipino houseworkers, almost exclusively women. The space itself was functional and clean, and everything it contained served a dual purpose. The telescopic head of the electric shower provided tap water for the adjacent sink. The butane gas bottle powered a portable stove and a single lightbulb. The wall-mounted banquette that ran the length of the room doubled as bed and chair to a little foldable table Wilson noticed resting behind the wooden door. Even the key Marianne had given him acted as a door handle. Apart from his room, the key also opened a single Turkish toilet cubicle shared by all occupants. Inside, the smell of latrine was eye-watering. Only a few weeks, he told himself, making a mental note to use the toilets downstairs.

From the rooms, he accessed the flat via a narrow wooden staircase. No carpet there, he noticed. Instead, the walls were marked by decades of occupants dragging heavy loads up and down worn-out stairs speckled with stains.

The next morning, he galloped his way down and knocked on the kitchen door. Conchita opened, still guarded.

"Charlotte!" she called.

The little girl emerged, a large smile on her face, and insisted on showing him every trinket in her parents' living room, as if the objects bore a significance beyond the fact that they acted as mementos from past family trips. He'd wondered whether she gave the tour to every new visitor or whether he'd been given some sort of special treatment, a response to the exoticism he must have represented in this Parisian household, and which the girl must have instinctively recognised. The comedic vision of a Russian painter depicting a tall African woman walking a fly on a lead had infused him with a certain reserve at first, but the girl's enthusiasm was contagious. He decided to give the family a chance.

After breakfast, Charlotte dragged Wilson to the play park that hung below the Trocadero. He was glad for the familiar space, although mid-week the place was hardly recognisable. The tourists had dispersed, replaced by locals walking small, pampered dogs and nannies pushing prams laden with colourful buckets and tools destined to entertain their charges. Two blonde children played in the sandpit, building a castle under the watchful eye of a woman sat on a bench. Wilson assumed she was foreign, on account of her sleek jet-black hair. He smiled in her direction, walking towards the bench, but as soon as she saw him, she pinned her gaze on the sandy children, holding her bag firmly on her lap. Charlotte called then, and Wilson walked towards the seesaw on which she sat.

"*Joue avec moi*," she pleaded, pointing at the other seat.

Wilson rocked up and down with Charlotte on the seesaw, pushed her on the swing, rescued her from the large metal frame when she got stuck, and lifted her on his shoulders, running around the sandpit, arms outstretched, pretending to be a plane. When he ran past the bench, he noticed that the nanny had collected her things and was dragging the two children away. Oblivious,

Charlotte urged him on, "Encore! Encore!" giggling with delight. Afterwards, they continued to the Esplanade, stopping to watch the water cannons shooting droplets into the air.

"Look, a rainbow," Wilson showed Charlotte. "The water is refracting the light."

"*Arc-en-ciel*," she replied with a huge grin, placing her small hand in his.

They walked like that all the way to school, skipping as they went along. At the school gate, Charlotte threw her arms around Wilson and hugged him tight before running onto the playground.

In the afternoon, Wilson explored the neighbourhood, watching the ballet of women pulling little caddies in and out of shops. They were buying golden baguettes wrapped in thin paper from the bakery, generous cuts of meat from the butcher, and pointed at colourful vegetables spread on wooden stalls, that a man dressed in a blue coat weighed and placed in brown paper bags. Shopkeepers greeted customers. Women stopped mid-pavement to exchange a few words, and although Wilson could not understand a word, he felt a surge of familiarity as he recalled his father's courtyard at home. There was much that was different, yet at the same time, everywhere you went people were much the same, Wilson thought.

At five o'clock, he returned to the school entrance and collected a buzzing Charlotte. Together, they walked to the bakery where Wilson purchased an ice cream cone with the money Marianne had left him that morning and handed it to Charlotte. From there, they continued to the Ranelagh Park. It was different from the rather functional-looking Trocadero gardens. A white gravel alley stretched around a large, manicured lawn delineated by flower borders. Across the lawn from where they stood was a wooden structure in front of which rows of children huddled on miniature benches painted forest green. Charlotte pulled at Wilson's sleeve. "It is about to start."

Wilson nodded and stepped onto the grass, immediately stopped in his tracks by a piercing sound. Charlotte said something he failed to understand. Turning towards her, he noticed a man in a navy-blue uniform marching towards him, a whistle still in his mouth. He blew a second time, drawing an insistent finger towards a little rectangular sign planted amongst the flowers, showing a crossed-out shoe. Wilson understood and stepped back onto the alley. The park officer had reached Wilson and Charlotte by then and pulled out a white notebook and a pencil from his inner jacket pocket. He proceeded to write up what Wilson realised was a fine. Bewildered, Wilson held the limp piece of paper the officer handed him, whilst Charlotte picked a handful of coins from his hand and gave them to the officer who stored them in a little bag secured around his waist.

"We can walk around," she added, grabbing Wilson by the hand, and directing him towards the marionettes stand. Wilson sat side-by-side with lines of children roaring at the character of Guignol, a mischievous wooden puppet playing tricks on a gendarme, hitting the officer of the law on the head with a large wooden stick.

Afterwards, Wilson walked Charlotte home and returned to his room, wondering what sort of place fined people for stepping on the grass whilst entertaining children with puppet shows in which the common man fought back against police violence.

The visa to the States never came.

3. DISPERSION

Wazungu

The local school I attended was private, frequented by children of diplomats, lawyers, and investment bankers, many of whom could trace their French family roots back to Charlemagne. I took ballet classes, learnt to play the piano, curtsied in front of respectable grandmothers; silently greeted guests, taking their coats, offering them appetisers on little silver trays; always sitting quietly, back straight, knees pressed together.

Then, halfway through primary school, my mother hired a Nigerian babysitter, and it was as if two worlds collided.

"Shall I give you the tour?" I asked Wilson the first time we were introduced, as if the grown man needed my guidance. I pointed at the furniture in the lounge – a lacquered table from China with embedded mother-of-pearl herons that had belonged to one great-grandmother or another; some heavy-set silver bracelets turned into ashtrays which my mother had purchased in Morocco; a picture book about Quetzalcoatl with photographs of feathered totems from Central America. I noticed he raised an eyebrow at a painting of a tall African woman walking a fly on a lead. The artist was a Soviet in exile, I said then, parroting what I'd heard my father tell other visitors.

If my mother ever considered what Wilson would make of this exotic display of family heirlooms, she didn't let it show. As for me, I treated Wilson as a long-lost older brother. He embraced every make-believe game I came up with wholeheartedly, walked me to the Esplanade after school, patiently taught me how to roller-skate. For days, he held my hand and broke my fall until I was steady enough to skate alone. Most of all, he let me watch films late into the night whenever my parents went out. I adored him.

There were looks. Most met the presence of Wilson with a disapproving frown to which my mother responded with light humour. A few asked if she had lost her mind: "A man sitter? What were you thinking?" they'd said, their eyes pointing at the colour of his skin. One, a haughty woman with a severe haircut who lunched at the Paris Tennis Club, and holidayed in Deauville, asked about the sort of influence such an individual could have on the children.

"We were looking for an English-speaking sitter," my mother replied, in a measured tone. "As for the inference, I was raised by loving African nannies. I don't think I turned out too bad."

"Still," the woman pressed. After that, there was no further playdates with her children.

"Their loss," my mother said. Overall, she ignored those women, pretending not to see their wagging fingers. I could see how she, too, considered Wilson a part of the family. We both felt at ease in his presence. He talked about growing up in Nigeria, free to roam the countryside with his siblings after school. Under the pretext of teaching Wilson French, my mother shared with him stories of a different kind of childhood. To him, she spoke of all the places she had lived. In exchange, he taught her words in Yoruba and Swahili, like precious birds he held in his hands, passing them on so they could soar. He named her *Wazungu*. The word for wanderer.

Bordeaux

A month after the trip to Utah, I boarded a train to Bordeaux, a five-hour ride, away from everything I knew. I was eighteen years old, convinced my life in Paris was over. In the peculiar way of my family, we had travelled far and wide whilst I was a child, yet I'd never been to Bordeaux, or any big French cities outside of Paris, for that matter. Naive, I imagined the wine city as a blank canvas on which I could paint a life for myself. The university offer had come as a welcome response to a desperate need to distance myself from my parents and cut all ties with this Parisian society in which I had been raised and lost myself. I'd read the phone call from the registrar as a sign, an exit route from the anguish of others' judgements, and the repressed and all-consuming anger I felt towards my mother, which grew more irrational by the day. I'd joined my parents in the kitchen, announced I'd be leaving the next morning, packed a bag with only a few clothes. I didn't tell anyone else I was going. I simply slipped away.

Walking from the train station up Cours de la Marne, to the city centre, I stopped to look at the window of an estate agent, unsure how to proceed. After a minute, I pushed the glass door open and entered. Inside, a woman in a red tailored suit looked up. "Can I help you?"

"I'm looking for a place to live," I said, adding that I had been accepted as a student in the university and was due to start there the following day.

"It is late to be looking," she said. "Most of our student flats have gone by now." She paused to think. "I might have something." Grabbing a set of keys from her desk, she invited me to follow her back onto the street, and a few hundred metres back in the direction of the station I had arrived from. "This one just came in. The parents had bought the bedsit for their sons. Now that they've all graduated, they are looking to rent."

The bedsit was on the ground floor, a single room carpeted in navy-blue tiles from floor to ceiling, rescued from total darkness by large glass panels, frosted, in the middle of which stood a door opening onto a concrete courtyard. Through there, natural light flooded, lending the space the air of an artist's studio. The layout itself was simple. A mezzanine bed, a sofa, a kitchen sink, and a table on which stood an electric hob.

"The bathroom is next door," the estate agent clarified, although I hadn't thought to ask.

We exchanged the keys an hour later. This would be the place in which I would grow a life for myself, I thought. Equidistant from the train station that carried me back to Paris at weekends, and the city centre from where I could catch a bus to the campus in Talence. It seemed perfect. Later I'd found out that on warm days creepy crawlies swarmed into the flat, from the other side of the wall. Propping a chair against the grey breeze blocks, I hoisted myself up to take a peek. I found a small rectangular piece of what appeared to be wasteland at first, overgrown with brambles and colourful weeds. Then I noticed the carved slabs under the wild vegetation, worn out, ancient. A caterpillar trailed over my hand, its scurrying feet sending a shudder down my spine. I tried to shake it off, lost my balance, and fell hard on my back. For a moment, I imagined the earth over the wall, rich with decomposed bodies. I stared at a line of ants chasing an invisible scent inside my flat, as if I, too, belonged with the corpses.

At night, I hardly slept. As I turned off the light, unfamiliar sounds drowned me into a panic. Gripped by a developing sense of paranoia, I spent each night flashing a light in the direction of the back door's lock from my mezzanine bed, checking and re-checking that I had indeed secured it shut.

In the day, I set out early to explore, discovering a bakery open 24/7 and the wholesale market, which stood across the road from my place. Attracted by the early cacophony, I watched as a man in a flat cap and grey workman's coat stood behind a pulpit, calling out produce in a fast repetitive melody that reminded me of a jig, only interrupted by the merchants shouting their proposed prices in response. Afterwards, I walked to a square surrounded by bars, their terrasses stretched onto the pebbled pavement, identical venues only distinguished by the mismatched colours of their large awnings, tensed canvases shading the seating area. Red. Green. Blue. Partly obfuscating a series of bus stops, erected like a quirky urban forest, a nerve centre for all transport in and out of the city.

There, I would spend four years, travelling daily to Talence, a small town on the periphery of Bordeaux. Following in my father's footsteps. Studying what he had studied. Learning independence; mostly how lonely it felt, how desperate I was to integrate into a community of my own. On campus, I watched other students with curiosity, not recognising myself in any of them. Most had come from small towns right across France, and on hearing I was from 'the capital' they displayed an immediate antipathy towards me, one I dismissed as a silly quirk at first, until I understood how ingrained their hatred of all things Parisian really was. The author Jean-François Gravier had written his seminal book *Paris et le Desert Français* by then – Paris and the French Desert – and everyone in France had absorbed the message that France was resolutely metropole-centric.

"All you Parisian hate us people from the periphery," I heard a drunken student slur at a party, pointing in my direction.

"I'm not sure that's true," I'd replied, moving towards the group he was addressing, defensive. They seemed unconvinced. "Mostly, we don't care," I'd blurted out.

My unwise comment spread, and I fell victim to a blanket silent treatment after that, the little social life I had had turning into its very own desert.

In the course of that first year, I went from visiting my parents every weekend, to every other, and eventually only for the major holidays.

I withdrew into myself in the little navy-blue bedsit which seemed to me to grow darker with every passing day. Eventually, I realised I needed urgent company, and looked for a shared accommodation. I moved into a two-bedroom flat on Cours Pasteur with a student from Morocco and her Algerian boyfriend. The place was dark, damp, its layout tortuous. The main flat was on one level, whilst my room and the bathroom were under the rafters. Aïsha told me that when they'd first moved in her boyfriend had found stacks of old mattresses in the room, a sure sign, he had told us, that the place had once been occupied by illegal migrants. Still, the rent was cheap and the location convenient since it was directly on the route of the Talence bus. The only commerce here was a sex shop, on the other side of the road, and a cloud of prostitutes, imports from West Africa, rooted to the bus shelter from where they operated at night, under the watchful eye of a man I guessed to be their pimp. Strangely, I never felt unsafe walking amongst them to catch the bus to university in the morning. My arrival marked the end of their shift, and they welcomed me with songs of blessed mornings and laughter, whilst their pimp seemed to vaporise at the first hint of light. I knew their names and they knew mine. Together we formed a curious little community, looking out for one another. Often, I wondered what had pushed them to leave their homes to come here, and whether, when they'd first arrived, any of them had squatted in the room where I now spent my nights.

In year three, Aïsha and her boyfriend broke up, prompting her to trade Bordeaux for Paris. Unable to cover the rent on my own, I moved to a place in the Moroccan quarter owned by one of Aïsha's distant uncles. It was a part of Bordeaux where the smell of kebab meat and hashish constantly filled the air, mixed with the calls of men selling crockery and *kesra* bread to send money back to the *bled*. Living there, I felt a strong sense of the familiar, accompanied by the joyous undulating tunes of *raï* singers blaring from little transistor radios.

Aïsha's uncle kept watch over me like a protective parent, carrying out repairs and ensuring I stocked my refrigerator with fresh fruits and vegetables. My parents, by contrast, felt increasingly distant.

My mother and I spoke on the phone. Rarely. Briefly.

My father sent formal emails about sound budgeting to fund my studies, and envelopes of magazine clippings, recipes he thought I could use to socialise with the new friends he assumed I had gained: cauliflower salad in aïoli sauce, stuffed cabbage in red wine, grilled *dorade* on a bed of fennel. Traditional French recipes, at odds with the tajines and *keftas* I associated with the home-cooked food from my childhood.

The remainder of my time there dissipated in clouds of hashish supplied by an enterprising neighbour.

Taormina

To celebrate the end of my time in Bordeaux, my mother had arranged an organised trip to Sicily. Confined to a coach several hours a day, I listened, bemused, as she laid out her plans for my return to Paris. She had already lined up a job for me, she said, calling in favours through my father's relations. She had pre-selected apartments for me to look at.

"I can help you with the decorating," she added.

"What about my plans?" I replied, defensive.

We argued from Palermo to Marsala. From Marsala to Syracuse. From Syracuse to Taormina. There, we witnessed elderly Sicilian women in black dresses brushing grey ash into neat little monticules. As we approached Mount Etna, the smell of sulphur filled our nostrils, giving the air an almost powdery consistency. Everywhere, a monochrome wave of black magma had coated the land, robbing it of shape and colour. We climbed up, silenced by the desolation. As we reached the top, my mother exploded. "You throw away everything I do for you," she shouted, her voice carrying past me into the void.

"Has it even occurred to you I might want to make my own choices?" I screamed back.

She shrugged. Her tone was soft again. Defeated. "I don't understand you, Charlotte. Can't you be more like normal girls?"

I felt my blood rising. "Who are you calling abnormal?" I sighed. "There is nothing normal about you. You spent most of your life travelling the world, but I am forced to live out your little bourgeois fantasy, always polite, always quiet. Don't you see those people you want me to befriend are all fake?"

She held my gaze, shaking.

"I mean, growing up I had more genuine conversations with the housekeeper," I continued. "There has to be more to life than this endless performance!"

She turned her back on me then, scuttling down Mount Etna at such speed I could hardly keep up. All the way to Palermo, she didn't speak a word.

As soon as we landed, I walked onto the tarmac and into a taxi, leaving my mother behind. The taxi dropped me off outside our Paris flat. Realising I no longer had the keys, I wandered for hours, walking under the archways of the overhead rail line – number 6 – to Montparnasse. Rue du Bac, I turned towards the Latin Quarter. It was a place filled with simpler childhood memories. We used to come here to the cinema with my parents, every Saturday, grabbing a cheese and ham crêpe from the street vendor on the rue de l'Odéon. I wasn't sure when it had stopped. Maybe around the time Wilson had left us. By the time I reached St Michel, the anger had partially receded, soothed by the sight of my beloved second-hand booksellers with their wooden boxes painted green, perched on the walls of the embankment. Their familiar symmetry marked the edge of the more bohemian Rive Gauche where I imagined my mother had spent so much time during my childhood whilst Dad was in work. I crossed the river and walked along the Seine, to the Quai d'Orsay.

At the door of the Ministry, I marched confidently to the security booth – someone who belonged – and asked to speak to my father. A few minutes later, a secretary, impeccably dressed, showed me in.

"Papa."

"Sweet pea. Your mother called," he said, with a frown of disapproval.

I raised up my hands in surrender, cocking my head to one side. "I don't understand why she must shoehorn me into this *persona*. Why can't she just let me be?" I recounted my version of the exchange, knowing my mother would have presented a very different perspective. "How shallow can she be, right?" Deep down, I knew my father always took my side anyway. It was us against the world.

"You should have more respect for your mother," he replied.

"Respect is something you have to earn," I replied, half in a whisper. "Anyway, I've come to rescue you," I announced, louder. "Let's go get food together, petit papa."

I adored my father to the point of blindness, ignoring the way he spoke about his female colleagues, as if they were a bunch of incompetent idiots conniving to take credit for others' work. Part of me excused him, refusing to admit this misogyny was more than ingrained bravado, a hangover from a military upbringing. I saw myself following in his footsteps, incapable of processing the contradiction that his encouragements implied, driven instead by an irrational need to prove myself his equal. He worked as a ministerial advisor, specialised in economic development; spoke fondly of the many projects he oversaw to encourage a francophone partnership with *nos amis africains*. Our African friends, that's how he referred to them. A war orphan, he believed in the French ideals of the Republic: meritocracy, universalism, and the continuous *mission de coopération* which France shouldered with its former colonies. He painted a compelling picture.

We arrived at his favourite café in the Latin Quarter, *Les Deux Magots*, a stone's throw away from St Germain church. We took a table at the terrace, ordered an omelette and a glass of red.

"It is as if she doesn't think I am able to achieve anything on my own," I complained, continuing my internal monologue out loud. I stopped, noticing the way his eyes hooked onto the passers-by, following them for a while, lingering on women's calves, guessing at others' lives.

"Earth to Dad, are you still with me?" I laughed, forgetting my anger.

He turned towards me and smiled. "She is just trying to make things easy for you."

I shrugged.

"What do you plan on doing then?"

I pulled out a leaflet from my bag and handed it to him. As he read, I told him about the Erasmus programme, about the opportunity to get some much-needed distance, to emulate the rest of my family by travelling to another country, gaining new perspective.

"Do you think you can just go like that?" he said, sounding alarmed.

"Over there, I can find myself without constant interferences," I told him.

He nodded and dug into his omelette. I ate mine with a chunk of baguette, scoffing the fluffy eggs as if it was a race, all the while eyeing him, waiting for his verdict. He cleared his plate first, raised his glass.

"To your journey then. *Bi-smi llāh.* Come back to us soon."

Our glasses clinked. This is it, I thought. Freedom.

Charles de Gaulle Airport

A month later, my mother drove me to the airport to catch a flight to Cardiff, *Pays de Galles*.

"I have a surprise for you," she said in the car.

I sank into the car seat, looking ahead at the traffic build-up. Just don't make me miss my flight, I thought.

In the airport terminal, I spotted Wilson in a navy-blue Air France suit coming down the escalator, a broad smile on his face. He looked older, a few strands of silver lending him the air of a dignitary. The three of us embraced like long lost relatives.

"Do you have time for a coffee?" he asked me.

"Of course," I replied.

He led the way to the nearest café, pointing at shops, guiding us past offices, as if the airport was his private domain. The three of us sat at a little round table. Wilson insisted on getting the drinks, then whilst we were waiting, he pulled out two pictures from his wallet.

"My children," he qualified.

The glossy paper revealed two chubby toddlers in yellow and green dungarees outside a freshly painted bungalow. L'Haÿ-Les Roses, he clarified, a nice suburb in the Val-de-Marne. The second picture showed Wilson in traditional Nigerian dress standing next to a tall woman with chestnut hair and deep blue eyes, wrapped in an elegant golden dress.

"My wife Sonia," Wilson said, smiling. "She teaches French. That's how we met."

"And Wilson completed a business degree, you know." My mother interjected.

Wilson nodded. "I've been Head of Customer Services for Air France, here at the airport, for several years now," he said, straightening his back and smiling in the direction of my mother as if seeking her approval. "It is a good job."

He had lived near Bougival for a while, later moving to a bigger house with his family. Twice a year they took a trip back to Nigeria.

"It has been hard for my mother, me not going back," he frowned. "She is happy for me of course, but she misses having us all around, especially since my father passed." He cleared his throat with a dry cough.

"Does Sonia like Nigeria?" my mother asked.

"I think so. But you know ... to her, it is an exotic holiday. She's been trying to learn Yoruba phrases, familiarise herself with my people's customs."

"Sure," my mother said, placing her hand on his.

"Anyway, I'm a French citizen now. Who would have thought, right?" He tilted his head, and for a moment something passed between the two of them. Then Wilson composed himself and turned towards me.

"And here you are, Charlotte, starting your own adventure. You must be very excited?"

I shuffled on my seat. "It's only for a year, you know. Trying to get a flavour of something different."

The airport Tannoy sounded then, calling for Cardiff passengers to board.

"Sorry we don't have more time," I said, grabbing Wilson's arm. "It's been so good to see you."

"Time to catch that flight," my mother said, straightening her skirt as she stood up. "Will you walk us?"

The three of us made our way to the bottom of the escalator leading to the boarding gates in silence. There, my mother handed me my bag and we said goodbye, without exuberance, as if I was popping out to the bakery. Wilson, by contrast, wrapped me in both arms and lifted me off the floor. "Safe trip, Little Shrimp," he whispered as he returned me to the ground. Whilst the mechanical steps carried me away, I turned to look at the peculiar pair. They stood at a polite distance from one another, straight as two pillars, the pillars of my childhood.

The Journal

I turned the book several times in my hands, intrigued by the title that bore my name, finally opening it onto an empty page of thick-grained orange paper.
"It is empty," I remarked, puzzled.
"It is a travel journal," my mother said.

Three days before my flight to Cardiff, television screens around the world had broadcasted two planes crashing into the Twin Towers. At the time, I was drinking coffee and chain-smoking in my parents' kitchen with my best friend Aline who had come to say goodbye. We were joking about the quantity of anaemic baked beans and fish drowned in vinegar that I would have to ingest, *en Angleterre*; stereotypes acting as a reassuring anchor when one is faced with the unknown. The phone had been ringing all day, family members calling to extend their goodbyes, behaving as if I was on the verge of an expedition in the deep jungle of Peru. The phone rang again, and I picked up the receiver with joyful anticipation.

"Switch on the TV," my auntie Elizabeth's voice bellowed, a full pitch higher than usual. "World War Three has started." Her cryptic message delivered, she hung up, leaving me standing with the receiver in one hand, mouth agog.

"What's happened?" Aline asked, sensing a crisis.

"I don't know. The TV," I replied, waving her in the direction of my parents' bedroom. Aline and I sat, side by side, on the edge of the double bed, staring at recordings of a plane crashing into one of the Twin Towers, then a second, playing on a loop. Towers turning into columns of fumes. Images of small dots the shape of human beings falling through shattered windows, floating down as if in slow motion, disappearing off-screen, their blurry fate replaced by the perplexed face of a TV presenter on the ground, looking up, holding on to his earpiece, muttering a bewildered commentary amongst mounting clouds of what looked like more smoke. Concrete dust, he clarified, from the buildings above. Mixed with bone dust, we would later find out. Off-camera, the cries of invisible onlookers conveyed how we were supposed to feel, a mixture of panic and disbelief. We stared at the screen as if time itself had paused, looped into twenty-minute segments. Then my mother arrived from work, earlier than usual, and told Aline she had better go home. I walked back with her, commenting on what we had just witnessed, throwing conjectures about foreign attacks and government conspiracies, unable to comprehend the magnitude of what was happening. Outside Aline's apartment building we hugged, two friends who had grown into each other's life since kindergarten.

The enormity of this day seemed to mirror another which had happened five years before. One I couldn't even articulate to myself, but which was pushing me on. The world around me was dissolving, and I had lost the capacity to express in words how that made me feel. How anything, made me feel. As I packed that day, I placed the journal in a wooden box and closed the lid on this repository of a childhood that seemed to belong to someone else.

Cardiff

I landed in the UK on 14 September 2001.

At Charles de Gaulle Airport, the security staff narrowed their eyes at the elderly lady whose handbag contained green wool and knitting needles, confiscating the lot in the name of national security. A uniformed man sporting the Union Jack asked me if I was carrying nail clippers, waving in the direction of the plastic box from which a green thread had started to unravel. The request conjured up the instant image of a cartoonish character popping out of her suitcase like a Jack-in-a-box, armed with a minuscule nail clipper, leaping at the self-important man.

"Death by a Thousand Cuts," I murmured.

"You think this is a joke?" The guard took a step closer, hand hovering above his side-arm. What I saw in his eyes frightened me. A mix of righteous anger and frenzied panic. I watched as he pulled his weapon in slow motion, his face contorted into a mask as he took aim. My body shuddered in response to an imaginary discharge.

"No. Nothing sharp," I replied, my words hurried, feeling smaller than a pin. I scanned the content of my compact navy-blue suitcase as the man spread it out on the metal table. One green jumper, two pairs of socks, two plain t-shirts, and a long flowery skirt, a toiletries bag in sturdy brown canvas labelled Pan Am – a present from my mother, remnant of a different era of travel. Lastly, all my underwear. Eyes fixed on me; he ran his searching fingers amongst my clean knickers. Shaken, I averted my eyes.

"Go," he said after what felt like several minutes.

I gathered my things *pêle-mêle* into the suitcase, and fled towards the departure lounge, feeling sick at the thought of the man's invasive hands.

Beside me, there were only two people boarding the small A319 plane, destination Belfast via Cardiff. The needle-less knitting lady, and a

76

man in jeans and a t-shirt who didn't appear to carry any luggage. We were each herded to our seats, at a safe distance from one another. The plane took off in complete silence, none of the usual announcements having taken place, as if the crew was enacting a form of corporate grief. I felt numb, unable to associate the images still populating every newspaper and every TV screen with the experience of sitting in this aircraft. I think I fell asleep. An hour later, the jolt of the landing gear being released woke me. I watched the ground coming towards me as the plane landed at Cardiff International Airport. When I heard the de-pressurising sound, I stood and grabbed my suitcase off the luggage compartment, the rustling of my raincoat too loud as I progressed the length of the corridor. Neither of the other two passengers had moved. They would be continuing to Belfast, and so, miraculously, the plane had landed just for me.

At the bottom of the metal steps, the tarmac glistened with rain, reflecting the sky like a mirror. I made my way through a sliding gate marked 'A' and nervously trotted along a never-ending grey corridor lit up too brightly with halogen tubes, all the while holding my breath. As I passed a set of fire doors, I exhaled, looking around for any sign of life, only finding a line of deserted passport booths. I continued to the exit, unchecked, in search of transport. It was only when I reached the taxi rank that I encountered a tall man dressed in a square-shouldered suit. His head had a dusting of fine ginger hair, and his thick neck bore the red lines of someone accustomed to the outdoors. The man turned in the direction of my footsteps and offered a smile.

"Looks like we might need to share a cab," he said in a thick accent I was unable to place, pointing at the only taxi queued up. "Which way are you heading?"

"The university," I replied, weary.

"You can drop me off at the stadium on the way then," he said, reaching forward to open the car door. The gesture made me blink. I hesitated for a moment, considering the size of the man's hand, looking around for any other option.

"Are you getting in today?" a gruff woman's voice escaped from the driver's seat. Reassured, I stepped forward and took a seat. During the journey, the man and I exchanged information in the neutral way of strangers. He was in Cardiff for a meeting. I was due to start at university the following week. On hearing it was my first time in Wales, he offered to take me out for dinner. The invitation elicited an instant tightness between my shoulders.

"You're very kind," I told him, "But the journey has been tiring. I better not."

He smiled, graciously I thought. A few minutes later, the taxi dropped him off outside the large Millennium Stadium, an oval creature suspended in mid-air, perched along the river, faced by symmetrical lines of identical houses, red brick, slated roof, red brick, slated roof, as far as the eye could see. Shortly after, the road opened onto the fortified walls of Cardiff Castle, and the white stones of what I would come to know as the Civic Centre. The lady driver pointed at City Hall, the National Museum of Wales, and behind us, Cardiff University, where I would spend the next twelve months as an Erasmus student.

Years later, I would learn the man I had shared a cab with was a famous rugby player, and although I have never managed to remember his name, in time I came to associate his friendly demeanour with the people of Wales. After all, I would tell my mother on the phone, the Welsh were as welcoming and uncomplicated as the French were argumentative. I cringed at the oversimplification. There would be many others. As people often asked how I had ended up in Wales, I would quickly learn to rehearse a few acceptable standard responses. The truth, of course, is never that obvious.

As I look back, the memory of that day feels imprinted into my mind with photographic clarity. The stout little woman from the hall of residence who turned me away, hair pulled into a tight bun, face framed by giant golden earrings. Most of all, the way she pressed her lips in a motion I would later recognise as a typically British expression, a sort of weird self-censorship that prevented people from ever truly speaking their mind, forcing them to wear their disapproval as a constipated mask.

"Your room will be ready tomorrow," she had insisted, her tone final. After all, who turned up early to their own life? Retreating into the street, I walked back towards the city centre, ending up surrounded by dirty roses sewn on the ancient wallpaper of a B&B on Cathedral Road. I stared in wonderment at the little plastic tray on which stood an electric kettle, equipped with teabags, sachets of instant coffees, and single plastic pots of milk. I had been less impressed by the portable electric shower placed *à même* the dusty carpet, and the trickle of tepid water it had produced when I had attempted to use it. It didn't occur to me to go out and explore that first night, mostly because the presence of the kettle whispered to me that my host probably frowned at being disturbed. Maybe I should have given my travelling companion a number. In another life, I would have, but here I had hesitated, assailed by a sense of vulnerability. Here, I was anonymous, a potential nobody neither missed nor claimed. In any case, he had not insisted. Instead, I slipped under the cold duvet, displacing a cloud of dust that made me sneeze, and quickly fell asleep.

My first contact with *le Pays de Galles* was curated by an Erasmus coordinator who delivered 'British Society and Culture' in weekly segments that included a lesson on the rules of cricket, one on the writing of P.J. Hartley and a semester on the civilising power of the British Empire. Dressed in a creased grey suit and a pale blue shirt, his face bearing the marks of unrestrained exposure to sun and over-ingestion of alcohol, the man illustrated a series of statements with slides, personal pictures of his time in India: an attentive group of men in pressed Nehru shirts; villagers covered in bright pigments, celebrating the Festival of Light; a monstruous landslide in a more rural area. Most of all, he encouraged the group to listen to BBC

Radio 4's *The Archers*. "A programme that truly embodies the essence of what it means to be British," one of the German students parodied, sending a wave of laughter across the classroom. Apart from the compulsory module which counted for sixty credits, I had to pick two more. I decided on a double module titled Spanish conversation, reasoning that since I already spoke the language, it would leave me plenty of time to explore. The class turned out to be comical, since none of the other students dared speak to the buoyant Andalusian module leader, for fear of ridicule. Conversation turned into dialogue, and after a while we forgot the twenty pairs of eyes travelling from the colourful teacher to me as we exchanged lively commentaries about all that was strange to us here.

For the most part, being an Erasmus was a social activity. My housemates were an international bunch united by one imperative: to be entertained. We forgave the uneven pavements (you can't help the rain), accepted the damp houses and the faulty plumbing (it's student life for you). We existed as an island, organising house parties, walking to the cinema in a pack. Our number made us feel part of a global community, allowing us to forget that none of the British students had ever extended an invitation to any one of us. We had come to immerse ourselves into a new culture, only to be politely ostracised.

Determined to change that, I opened my laptop one day to search the list of clubs and societies offered by the Students' Union, thinking this might be a way to meet genuine British students. Across the Cardiff University Rambling Society page was a red banner: ACTIVITIES SUSPENDED UNTIL FURTHER NOTICE DUE TO FOOT-AND-MOUTH. I closed the lid and walked to the shared bathroom to apply make-up. I had been invited by a Greek student to a party in one of the rat-infested terraced houses at the back of the Union. He hadn't specified a time, but a few months attending Erasmus parties had taught me that the German students usually arrived first and brought beer. Us French followed, an hour later with a bottle of wine and some cheese. The

Spanish and Italian emerged after 10.00 pm and brought platters of salami. The Greek students, on the other hand, trickled in after midnight and took over the kitchen. Away from home, we had slipped into those stereotypes, enacting a sort of parody of ourselves, as if the act provided us with a protective cover, a veneer of exoticism. By contrast, I noticed, my British flatmates headed straight to the pub after class, staying until the bell rang at 11.00 pm. They seldom ate in the pub though. Only packets of cheese and onion crisps, or the odd plate of chips. I found the habit mystifying. To a French person, wine was best consumed with a good meal. Few of my flatmates could cook. They waddled back to the hall, burnt bread under the grill, and invariably triggered the smoke alarm. Meanwhile, my baked aubergines with cheese were met with incredulity. I considered recording those observations into a new notebook like I had done so many times before, comments about the curious language that occupied the bottom half of every street sign here, and echoed, although rarely, in university halls.

It would be a year before I could travel to the Brecon Beacon National Park with the Rambling Society. The Union minibus took us from Cardiff, travelling north on the A470, a gullet east of the Rhondda, drilled through the heart of communities shaped by 150 years of coal mining.

"People here have been robbed of their identity by Thatcher," the guide, a lecturer in City Planning, told us, adding that Welsh people held English policies responsible for drowning entire villages into life-long unemployment, a fact symbolically illustrated by a valley that had once been flooded to provide electricity to Liverpool. He assured us that the church steeple was still visible today. I thought I understood something of that sense of anger and loss he described. Mostly, his commentary conveyed a world of chapels, choirs, strong family ties, and Italian ice cream parlours. Happy vestiges of a once vibrant community of migrants from across Europe, attracted by the promises of industrialisation. The reality was rows of identical grey houses colonising hills to the east; purpose-built to accommodate the several generations of miners who had made the wealth of South Wales. The road climbed steeper after Merthyr, until we reached a bend. There, the guide pointed at a large rock on the side of the road. An oblong sign marking the entrance to the National Park. I had hoped for green trees and lush valleys, but looking around, all I could see were rocky hills, bare and yellow for miles. The odd flock of sheep roamed the dry landscape.

"We have reached farming country," the guide announced. "Let me take you through the Public Rights of Way before we arrive."

Scanning the slopes either side of the bus, I wondered how hills could look so burnt in a place that appeared almost constantly battered by the rain. It seemed a far cry from the green grasses of Wales we had studied in William Blake's poem. Here again, there was nothing that I could lay down on the pages of a travel journal.

Cartagena

Opening the envelope Madame Dubois had handed her, Marianne checked its contents. Cash. She made her way to Harrods, found a table, ordered a cup of tea. The umbilical cord with Morocco had been severed, but Marianne didn't know anyone here and soon the money would run out. Her priority was to find lodgings, and a job. What could a nineteen-year-old French girl do in 1962 London? Walking down Kennington Road, a brightly coloured sign caught her eye. A poster, advertising an air hostess training programme. In only a few pictures, the ad sold glamour, opulence, and the jet-setting lifestyle Marianne had so craved. Stepping into a red phone box, Marianne leafed through a copy of the Yellow Pages and located a boarding house in Fulham. The place was run by a widowed Glaswegian. The elderly woman agreed to rent Marianne a room at a discounted rate in exchange for a few hours of cleaning. The next day, she presented herself at the address on the poster, and registered for the training programme.

Marianne graduated a year later, a model stewardess part of an international team of young and elegant flight attendants hopping from one continent to the next. She soon became recognised for pre-empting the needs of a modern army of grey-suited men said to be building modern trade routes that would facilitate a new kind of entrepreneurial wealth. Marianne and her colleagues represented a secret weapon in a global campaign that brought class and exclusivity to international airlines. A Spanish speaker, she was offered a post with Avianca, the national Colombian fleet, to work long-haul flights from Bogotá. The atmosphere on the crew was professional but jovial. The other members were well-presented women from all nationalities, all speaking at least two languages other than their own, all filled with dreams of being swept away by an affluent passenger. At night, they met in sleek bars at international hotels where they drank colourful cocktails, compared mileage, and swapped stories in which boundaries between countries had long evaporated. This cosmopolitan crowd could be in Milan on a Monday, Singapore on a Wednesday and in Miami for Happy Hour. Wherever they went, they danced to the sound of Chubby Checker, Nat "King" Cole, and Ray Charles. The world was changing, and Marianne was at the heart of it all.

Every crew was led by a pilot. Some had army backgrounds, all had stories of impossible landings. The most famous was an Italo-Colombian who went by the name of Andres. Everyone had heard of him. The man was said to be able to land any plane, of any size, no matter the weather or the state of the runway. Marianne had heard from a senior colleague that he had landed a 747 on the Caribbean Island of Saba in the middle of a hurricane.

"This man is an artist," one of the other pilots had added. "Saba has one of the shortest runways in the world."

By the time her crew arrived at the hotel in Cartagena that night, Marianne felt weary. She checked in, showered, and lay on the hotel bed, staring at the ceiling. Despite all the fun, long-haul flights were hard on the system. Her legs had become prone to swelling, and she needed regular naps to combat the almost permanent jet lag.

When she woke, it was dark. Feeling refreshed, her legs rested, she unpacked her small suitcase, ironed her uniform ready for the morning. Glancing at the door, she hesitated. Pulling out a red satin dress from her luggage, she slipped it over her head, brushing the soft fabric with the flat of her hand. Climbing into a pair of high heels, she smiled at her own reflection in the mirror. What would Madame Dubois think of her now? She wondered.

The hotel bar was empty. Marianne sat on a high stool, placed her black velvet clutch bag on the counter and ordered a dry Martini. "Make that two," a deep baritone voice said behind her. "Is this seat taken?"

Marianne observed the man standing next to her. She guessed he was in his mid-thirties, handsome, his dark hazelnut eyes firmly locked on her face. She noticed he stood tall, exuding an air of authority.

"Let me guess. Pilot?"

He observed her with definite poise, taking his time. "*Muy guapa*," he said, taking her hand in his and brushing his lips against the soft part of her wrist.

Marianne felt heat bleeding across her cheeks. The sound of the barman shaking the cocktail startled her. She watched as he poured the translucent liquid into two glasses with measured movements. "Andres," the pilot introduced himself with swagger. He raised one glass. Handed her the other. "A toast?"

Marianne nodded, closing her eyes for a second.

"To love at first sight," he said.

"To love," she replied as if under a spell. She took the hand he was offering and followed this stranger onto the dance floor, filled with excited giddiness. For the first time in her life, she felt seen. They danced. They talked. Late into the night, they talked. Andres's mother was a seamstress from Cartagena who had died of consumption when he was a teenager. His father was a Sicilian captain, retired from the merchant navy. "He was rarely there. Always at sea," he told her. Andres had made his own way. Little jobs at first, plunger, cook, then thanks to an Italian restaurant owner from his father's village, pilot school. "An investment, the old man had called it." He took a deep breath. "Opportunities are everywhere if you know where to look, boy. That's what he used to say. He was right, too." Andres sounded so self-assured. That was the sort of man she had been waiting for, a provider, Marianne told herself, thinking of her aching legs.

"Meet me in Miami next week," he whispered as they parted that first night.

It sounded like a dare. Grasp this opportunity, a little voice resonated at the back of Marianne's head.

The following morning, she rang the management office, asking to be transferred to the Bogotá-Miami line. A week later, she was disengaging the plane locks and pushing open the door of the airplane onto the Miami runway. The silhouette of Andres waited for her on the tarmac, framed in the morning sunshine. Behind him, a blue 1962 Ford Thunderbird, fresh off the production line. "Fancy a ride?" He held the door as she hopped in and then he carried her suitcase to the boot. All day they drove the length of the city, admiring the opulent villas that lined the seafront. "I'll buy you one of those houses one day," he told her, and Marianne wedged herself in the fold of his arm, two bodies interlocked on the immaculate leather banquette. In the evening, he took her for dinner. Marianne recognised the name of the restaurant, one of those up-and-coming places the in-flight magazines wrote long articles about.

"I have to meet some friends," he told her afterwards. "Why don't you come with me?" He drove to the pleasure port of Miami, parked and made his way onto a pontoon that led to a large yacht, lit up in hundreds of colourful bulbs. A man in a cocktail jacket invited them to climb on board. The party was in full flow, accompanied by a live orchestra playing an energetic samba. Andres shook hands with a dozen, impeccably dressed men, handing cigars as he went. "Cuban," he specified, with a knowing smile.

Marianne paid little attention to Andres's dealings with those men, beyond the fact he spoke a back and forth of Italian and Spanish. Her attention was swayed by the women. Slender, beautiful women in designer dresses hooked onto their men's arm or moving voluptuously onto the dancefloor. What would the ladies from Harrods think of that? Marianne wondered. A waiter dressed in a white shirt and bow tie approached her, carrying drinks on a silver tray. "Champagne, Madame?"

Marianne took the flute that was offered and raised it in front of her. "To opportunities," she said before taking a sip.

"To opportunities, *mí guapa*," Andres replied, appearing out of nowhere, wrapping his arm around her waist and pulling her in for a kiss.

"How?" Marianne asked, gesturing at the wealth surrounding them.

"Let's just say that I'm a bit of an entrepreneur." He smiled. "Flying opens more doors than you think. This ... this life is ours for the taking Marianne." As he said it, he seemed to wave at the Miami night sky.

Andres spent more and more time with Marianne. Taking her for intimate dinners, bringing her to extravagant parties. She noticed he always brought gifts to his host, small, hard to obtain, tokens. Cigars from Cuba, or expensive alcohol, things she knew he must have smuggled in his suitcase. She pretended not to see. There was no harm. After all they all brought back things they weren't supposed to from time to time. Andres was working potential clients. She was determined to be supportive.

Months passed like that, in a blur. One day, Marianne found Andres on the runway, a smile on his face and a bottle of champagne in hand. "What are you doing here?" she asked, ushering him back to the arrival lounge. "You'll get us both in trouble."

"This is the one Marianne. The deal that will set us up for life. I did it," he said, handing her a flute and pouring the champagne. "And you, *mi guapa*, you are my lucky charm," he added. Staring deep into her eyes, he pulled Marianne's body closer and pressed his lips hard against hers. "I will never let you go."

Moving her head back a little, she took in the symmetry of his eyebrows, his high cheekbones, the fire in his expression. She could feel the tense muscle of his arm holding her tight. Losing herself in the intensity of the moment, she abandoned herself to him as they danced on the hot tarmac, surrounded by the heavy traffic of Miami International.

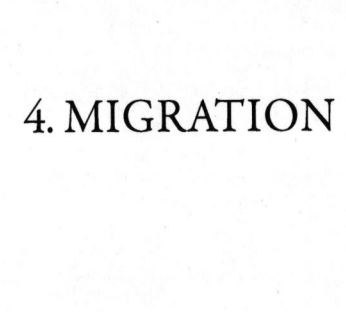

4. MIGRATION

Paris

West of Notre-Dame, la Colline de Chaillot was where I had grown up. It offered a raised vantage point from which the Parisian upper class surveyed the meandering life of a city that had evolved from swampy market town to cosmopolitan dreamscape. To the east, *la Colline de Montmartre* and its pearlescent dome contrasted with the memory of brothels and struggling artists inherited from centuries past. Nowadays they attracted droves of tourists to the capital. *So romantic.* So removed from reality.

I remembered the article my best friend Aline had sent about the bizarre epidemic that befell credulous Japanese tourists. Expecting Paris to exude sophistication, they had been confronted with a continuous assault of single-minded rudeness, pavements smeared with dog excrement, the screaming inanities of the street *clochard* sleeping off his *vin rouge* on underground vents outside the *Musée Asiatique*, vomiting a mixture of hot air and miasma which sprayed onto their impeccably tailored clothes. Traumatised, the Japanese travellers had to be repatriated without delay, deeply troubled by their experience.

I had laughed, unable to comprehend their naivety. I had had no expectation of Wales, which I would have been unable to place on a map before my trip. Retrospectively, *le Pays de Galles* would exist in cartoon form in my mind, a sister-bastion to the village in *Asterix le Gaulois* which the Romans repeatedly failed to submit. At first, I registered the similarities with Paris. A city built on marshland, turned interface between Industrial Britain and the rest of the world, supported by two rivers, the Ely and the Taff, and a profusion of coal travelling from the surrounding valleys.

I had assumed a similar opulence in Cardiff, with its castle and imposing Boulevard de Nantes coiling around the white-stoned civic centre that echoed the Parisian architecture of Baron Haussmann. The homogeneous buildings encircled Alexandra Garden, a manicured horticultural paradise flanked by symbols of power – City Hall, the National Museum of Wales, a courthouse, the Welsh Assembly Government, a university. Cardiff presented the veneer of an imposing capital city, heir to a time when Lord Bute had used his immense wealth to build the Docks and its surrounding rows of terraced houses. They had accommodated workers from the world over, men and their families, anxious to grab their share of the industrial dream. Their hopes were no different from that of my own family, hopping across continents in search of wealth and status.

I had failed to notice the piles of rubbish collecting in front gardens, or the misaligned concrete slabs that served as pavement. I knew nothing yet of the derelict buildings squatted by addicts along Newport Road, the hordes of homeless men fighting for a spot in the hedges of Alexandra Park, or the teenage prostitutes who emerged around the Magic Roundabout as night fell.

I lived in a place delineated by Canton to the west, and Cathays to the east. A place where student loans ensured a buoyant activity of estate agents, cafés, pubs, and clubs for at least nine months of the year. Most of all, I didn't notice because I came from the hill of Chaillot, a place of privilege, more Cyncoed than Butetown.

To me, the Thatcher era had been a single blurred image of a puppet set ablaze on the evening news. Only through walking in the Valleys would I start to take the measure of the impact of her policies on the mining community, and on its subsequent generations. In Cardiff, the after-effect on the dockyards had been eradicated by the construction of the barrage in 1999. By the time I came, Cardiff Bay was synonymous with showrooms for manicured apartments buildings, tended lawns, and allocated parking spaces.

Cathays

From the time I landed in Cardiff, my French eroded like the land, making room for a much-depleted version of myself, presenting to the world in imprecise English words that never quite defined anything with enough accuracy. It made me feel blurry around the edges, seeking new definition, lest I simply fade away.

It was the spring of 2003 before I thought again about capturing the big changes of my life on paper. Looking for shelter from the persistent Cardiff rain one day, I found myself in Royal Arcade. There was something comforting about this network of Edwardian and Victorian galleries below the imposing David Morgan department store. The place was at odds with the rows of British brands which I had come to associate with the High Street. In here, I felt a sense of calm, as if I had stepped into another time. I marvelled at the succession of distinctive independent shops selling vinyl records, unusual trinkets, and old photographic cameras. I reached The Pen and Paper, an appropriately named stationery shop. There, amongst shelves of colourful sketchbooks, lined notepads, and multi-purpose cahiers, I picked up a black notebook. A leather-bound 193 pages of acid free, virgin paper, weighty, reliable. From the expandable inner pocket, I pulled out a little leaflet titled 'A History of the Moleskine'. *A nameless object with a spare perfection all of its own, produced for over a century by a small French bookbinder who supplied the stationery shops in Paris, where artists such as Van Gogh, Picasso and Hemingway bought them*. A serious item, I thought, reading our common provenance as an omen. I envisioned the man who had bent over the first cover as he pressed blank pages together, and remembered the notebook from my childhood and the man who had made it. He still lived in Portugal. Despite my mother's exhortations, he had refused to make the journey to France for my grandmother's funeral. Some beef they must have had. Shrugging my shoulders, I placed money on the counter, and pocketed the notebook.

I walked straight back to Cathays where I lived, retracing my steps through the pedestrian part of the city centre, up Park Place, turning right towards Cathays Terrace in front of an abandoned petrol station which marked the corner of Maindy Road. Entering the house, I moved from room to room, exiting through the back door of the rented accommodation where I had decanted after the hall of residence. In the enclosed safety of the back garden, I took a deep breath, absorbing the late spring sunshine. I had been living on Maindy Road for a few years now, sharing with two architecture students who filled the house with a multitude of little tubes of glue. Glue for paper. Glue for cardboard. Glue for wood. Glue to seal ceramic to walls, to merge wood with metal into the shape of stairs, to place little tufts of green wool onto matchsticks to mimic trees. Tubes of glues, like potions, to magic cardboard cut-out lives which they hoped would lead them to fame, one day. The boys were nocturnal, spending all their time in the Studio – a mythical space on campus where architecture students disappeared from time to time, a hub of creative activity for a community of aspiring home creators amped up on life-and-death competition.

I enjoyed their absence. It gave me space to play-act a life unlike the one I had left behind. The garden was a novelty for someone who had grown up in a city apartment. I made it my mission to transform the bare patch of land and gravel into a lush lawn surrounded by tiger lilies, their speckled orange flowers contrasting with dangling fuchsias and the vivid blue of campanula muralis, clustered along the partition wall with the old, retired neighbour who liked to sunbathe in his underpants and, on hearing my accent, had insisted on telling me Hitler was a chap who had had a few good ideas in his time. I wasn't certain what to say to that, wondering if he had me confused with a German, or if in his mind us Europeans were all the same.

In those days, Maindy Road was still an industrial zone. Across the road was a succession of rectangular red brick buildings where exceptional load trucks brought train coaches for repair, mostly at night. I was amazed that one side of the house could overlook industrial workshops, whilst on the other I could step into nature and observe blue tits, wrens, and red robins perched on the blooming magnolia tree. I suppose this house aptly summed up the image I had of Wales.

Sitting on a pile of wood delineating the garden path, I opened the first page of the new notebook, clutched at my biro, and paused a moment. My old journal had contained details from childhood journeys and family anecdotes told and retold at bedtime, amplified by my imagination into mythical adventures. What did I have to write about my own travels so far? I wondered.

Eventually, I traced a few words on the lined page, in English. By then what had started as a gap year had turned into the sketch of a new life, like a diorama populated with an English boyfriend named Terry, a job in the university, and a shared house with a garden. My existence had gradually solidified into a (translated) version of itself, filling invisible cracks that belonged to a past that seemed increasingly foreign.

My Welsh self was like a sponge, or maybe more accurately a parasite; feeding from every experience, every word, every person I met, every place I visited. After just a few more years, I would make new friends, move to a flat in Cardiff Bay, marry Terry. Every day I leant forward into this life, stepping further away from my old one and from the cosmopolitan community that had provided a welcome safety net when I'd first arrived. I congratulated myself on how quickly I had assimilated, making a conscious effort to stay away from the diaspora of French expats on campus, immersing myself into what I mistook for authenticity.

Not long after I bought the new notebook, the nightmares started. I dreamt I was living in one of those architecture maquettes with the glued-on stairs and the matchstick trees. I would wake drenched in sweat, feeling destabilised on an almost atomic level. So much had changed in so little time, it was as if my appetite for novelty had waned from over-exposure. Without the elation, everything around me suddenly felt more and more staged.

In the pub after work, I would watch customers executing their strange ballet. I noticed the costumes they wore, men in 'smart jeans' with leather loafers, freshly ironed shirts, and the smell of cheap body spray and hair gel; women in high heels, tight jeans, and low-cut tops, hair dyed blonde and ironed flat. I noticed the dialogues they exchanged, men commenting on rugby, football, and the price of lager; women gossiping about office romance, holiday packages in Spain, and the latest bargain purchased off the rack. They moved around each other, seldom touching, as if steered by an indiscernible script; a highly gendered society where everyone understood their role. An alien society for someone who had grown up with mixed groups of friends who did everything together. The more I noticed, the further removed I felt. Of course, it showed. Feeling exposed, I elicited suspicion by declining a drink. Struggling to hear conversations made inaudible to my foreign ear by the hubbub of rugby supporters and shrill hen night laughter, I missed cues. Increasingly, I sat a little removed from the others, shoehorned into a role of anxious observer.

"*Voulez-vous coucher avec moi, ce soir?*" a drunken colleague mouthed into my ear one night, grinning with self-satisfaction at his clever usage of the Lady Marmalade lyric. I'd been sitting alone for a while at that point. I looked around, but nobody was paying attention to us. Feeling scared, I crossed my arms, hiding my body.

"Loosen up, love," he said in a sultry voice. "Can't you take a bit of harmless banter?"

I stood up to leave. He grabbed me by the wrist, a mean expression on his face. "You know, love, however long you stay, you'll always be the French girl. Get used to it."

I felt a huge surge rise inside of me, half-rage, half-panic, and pushed the man away with enough strength to land him against a table corner.

"Fucking mad cow!" he screamed. "Go back to your own country!"

I picked up my bag and coat and ran out. The cool air hit me in the face like a slap. I walked for an hour, reaching the dark waters of Cardiff Bay. I sat on a bench and stared at the unfocused space around me, willing that I could order my thoughts. Maybe the man was right. Life as a student in Cardiff had had the consistency of a welcome parenthesis at first, but maybe it was time to go home. Except I was no longer sure where *home* was. I felt detached somehow, like flotsam.

Paris

I was twelve when I unearthed my mother's jewellery box from the back of the wardrobe. A box which contained a brooch in the shape of airplane wings, a large pendant in a style I hardly associated with my mother, and a plain silver band. I picked up the ring to take a closer look, noticed a faded engraving. Two names. After I had read the names, I took the ring to my mother.

"Who is Andres, Mum?"

She took the small object I was handing her and sighed deeply.

Back in the bedroom, she placed the lacquered box on her lap and, using one hand to hold the mirrored lid, lifted the tray coated in deep red velour cloth, revealing a hidden compartment. From the concealed double bottom, she extracted a black and white picture on thick paper, more daguerreotype than snapshot, showing the handsome face of a young man, posing in uniform, carrying the aura of a cinematic icon. I grabbed the picture, avid with questions. Turning it around, I noticed ink markings on the back, a handwritten message in faded black script. Spanish. *Te quiero, Andres.* After a minute of uncomfortable silence, my mother finally spoke.

"I was married before your father. It was a long time ago. He wasn't a good man," she added, pre-empting any further questions.

"Wasn't? Past tense?"

Her face hardened then, as if a memory had cast its shadow.

"It is in the past. No reason to raise the dead. Your father wouldn't like us talking about it."

I watched as my mother lifted the picture from my hands and placed it back in the box, an innocuous relic she stored amongst old pairs of shoes. Afterwards, she went back to the kitchen, without as much as a word, or a glance. I remember feeling a deep sense of incomprehension then. A few minutes later, her voice called me to come set up the dinner table, our exchange erased, as if it had never existed.

Acapulco

On the morning of their honeymoon, Andres woke Marianne with a kiss. "I have to go out for a few hours, *querida*. An impromptu business meeting in the city."

Before Andres left, they shared breakfast in bed: he a black coffee with eggs, her a large glass of orange juice and a croissant. Between each mouthful of food they kissed, and smiled, staring deep into each other's eyes. Afterwards, he downed his drink and jumped from under the covers. "Time to get ready," he said, eyeing the direction of the bathroom. "You coming, Mrs?"

They made love hurriedly under the warm flow of water, then Andres wrapped Marianne in a thick hotel towel and stood her in front of the mirror. "You're all mine, *querida*," he said, holding her tight. She smiled in response.

"Will you be long?"

"Only a few hours, I promise. I'll escort you downstairs on my way out."

Marianne protested a little, but it was a glorious day to be sunbathing.

After he left, she worked all afternoon on perfecting her tan, sipping large Bloody Marys in long thin glasses decorated with brightly coloured little paper umbrellas. Laying on a long chair by the side of the pool, she remembered a conversation with her brother Jean. He had taught her that the French *transat* held its name from the deckchair found on transatlantic cruise ships, a place for wealthy passengers to catch a bit of sun and fresh air, preventing illness, whilst second-and third-class ticket holders remained below deck for the duration of the passing. Marianne suddenly felt worlds away from her childhood in Morocco. Andres had saved her, she thought. Checking the time on the hotel clock, she noticed he was running late. She had been by the poolside a few hours and her skin started to burn. She retreated to the nuptial suite to take a shower and cool herself off. It was about five by the time she came out.

Contemplating the room for a moment, she decided to go wait in the bar, a fitting *clin d'oeil* to their first meeting. She wrote a note and headed out.

In the dimmed light of the bar, sitting at the brass-polished zinc, she spied on couples, clustered around little round candlelit cabaret-style tables, deep in intimate conversations. She noticed her own bored reflection in the large behind-the-bar mirror framed with shelves, carrying a multitude of colourful bottles. Each seemed filled with exotic liquors, and, on the end of the bar, a young alchemist was mixing extravagant cocktails. Mesmerised, she pointed at a few preparations.

"Could I try this one?" she asked, hoping to strike up a conversation with the barman. His name was Eris. Like any good barman, he was engaging. He told her he was an archaeology student writing a thesis on pre-Colombian art. With his tanned face, tousled hair and encyclopaedic knowledge, he embodied the sort of travelling explorer Marianne had imagined from the nineteenth-century travel literature that populated her stepfather's shelves in Rabat. An adventurer in search of lost civilisations. They talked, and laughed, and drank, Eris's stories helping Marianne forget about Andres's absence.

It was midnight by the time she noticed her husband's reflection in the mirror. She was hazy from the cocktails, uncertain how long he had been standing there, observing. Too delighted to see her groom to feel angered at his lateness, she spun herself around on the little bar stool with a push of her heel, leant into him, and flung her arms around his neck, oblivious to the rigidly raised eyebrows staring back at her.

"My love, here you are. I've missed you so much."

Ignoring her effusiveness, he prised her arms off him with a strong grip, yanked her off the stool and marched her towards the elevator by the elbow, a puppeteer directing a rag doll. If customers at the tables witnessed the scene, everyone assumed a polite blindness.

In the privacy of the lift, he brought her face roughly towards his, lifting her chin to smell her breath.

"What were you playing at, *mujer*?"

"I was waiting for you. Where –" was all that she managed – before a nauseating feeling forced her to clamp her jaw shut. A feeling of injustice swelled in her chest, mixed with pangs of shame. Outrage made way to feeble apologies.

The lift door opened on an empty corridor decorated with pictures recalling the city. In front of her eyes floated a frowning portrait of Frida Kahlo. She took an unsteady step, trying to stabilise herself, searching for her husband's arm, his presence evading her. She stumbled forward. Behind her, a guttural sound rumbled, not what she associated with the man she loved. Before she could turn, Andres had clasped a fistful of her hair, a lever to pull her upright, forcing her towards the door of their suite. He entered, dropped her, sobbing, on the bed, then went to take a shower.

"Look what you made me do," he said, wiping his hand with a towel before closing the door.

Cardiff

"When are you coming home?" my mother would ask on the phone with increasing urgency. But the more she asked, the more evasive I became; clinging to the idea that as long as I was in Cardiff all of life's options remained available. I was in no rush to decide. The university ecosystem helped. My department was populated by a cosmopolitan bunch of staff, beneficiaries from the will of the EU to facilitate the movement of ideas. Staff and students from diverse nationalities roamed the halls, providing nuanced cultural perspectives that the university described on its brochure as an enriching environment, illustrated by pictures of mixed groups of students sat on a lawn, laughing. Even then, something felt staged about those pictures, as if the students had been selected for the colour of their skin rather than the programme they represented. In reality, in those days the majority of students was homogeneously white, despite their distinct nationalities.

Still, the relative diversity of academic life had normalised my foreignness, giving me the impression that I had found a place after all. And of course, there was Terry. I had found a martial arts class that advertised easy self-defence for all. I walked into the sports hall at Talybont North that first night, and into a rectangular room filled with attentive students in matching white suits, knelt in neat single rows, around a thick tatami, facing an older man whose rotund belly hung over a worn-out black belt. At his side was a younger, slimmer man, with a vivid blue belt that echoed the aquamarine of his eyes. Engaging, he waved me towards an empty spot. I sat as instructed, and the class began. The sensei spoke measured sentences in a calm tone, explaining that the class's intention was to equip us with a basic set of skills so that we could repel an attacker if needed. The focus, he insisted, was not to start a fight, but to know how to end one. We all bowed then, at his signal, stepped onto the mat, and formed two parallel lines, face-to-face. When I looked up, I noticed the blue belt standing opposite. He smiled and took a step towards me.

"Grab me by the throat," he instructed.

A little startled at the thought of placing my hands around this stranger's neck, I glimpsed left and right, noticing the other pairs had already begun.

"Eyes on me," my partner called. Hesitant, I crossed both hands on top of one another, and wrapped my fingers as instructed, feeling the even pulse of his carotid under my thumb.

"It goes like this," he said, motioning both his arms in the space between us. He executed a simultaneous windmill movement with both hands, up and away, trapping my arms under his armpits. Suddenly constrained, I felt my heart galloping off a cliff.

"Like a blooming flower," he interjected, easing his grip. We were very close then. I felt his warm breath on my face. My cheeks radiating. I tried to speak, but only emitted an incoherent mumble, distracted by the feel of his sinewed muscles against my bare skin.

"Terry. My name is Terry. Nice to meet you," he smiled, releasing me fully. There was a disarming innocence about his eagerness. I gave him my name, wishing he would hold on to me a little longer.

After the class, we all went to an Indian restaurant on City Road, a weekly tradition, I would soon discover. I joined the martial arts club the next day and started to train three times a week. The dojo had a strange quality to it, as if it were its own bubble. I felt safe there. Part of something. Surrounded by a community of students and public servants: two firemen and three mental health nurses. Terry, a university graduate, worked for the Benefits Office in the council, helping protect vulnerable clients at risk of losing their homes. He was sweet, funny, dedicated. He had a strange passion for broken things. He would buy odd objects at car boot sales, observe them, clean them, give them another lease of life. He made me feel like I mattered. We started to meet outside of the club. Took walks in the park. Went to the cinema once. I loved that he always insisted on walking me home. One night, after a dinner, he lingered by the door, leant in for a kiss. The texture of his tongue in my mouth made me recoil, but I stilled myself and forced a smile. I liked him. I didn't want him to think that I didn't. I pushed the feeling down and returned his kiss. After that, there were many more dates. Many more kisses. I went with the flow because as long as I was with Terry, I felt protected. And just like that, we were moving in together, planning a wedding, imagining a future together.

Then, my job at the university came to an end. I set out the task of developing a CV, following guidance from the university's Careers Service. Weeks turned into months. Two applications turned into ten, into fifty. Sixty-seven applications later, I was finally invited to my first job interview. The company was looking for a graduate with the ability to speak French and Spanish. On paper, the job fitted me like a shoe. I felt optimistic.

The appointment was in the morning, in a business park on the edge of town. From the Bay, I needed to take two different bus routes. Unfamiliar with the area, I set out early, making sure to arrive with time to spare. The office was in a modern glass tower building, its entrance guarded by a suited security guard behind a high reception desk.

"Here for the interview?" he asked, scanning my tailored dress.

I answered with a smile.

"Sign your name here," he pointed to a clipboard and a pen tied to its base with a little chain. "This way," he added once I'd replaced the pen in its holder. He directed me to a side room where a middle-aged woman dressed in black trousers and a white shirt invited me to sit in front of a computer. She reminded me of a stern headteacher.

"There is a pre-interview test," she explained, adding the instructions were on the sheet in front of me.

I shuffled on the office chair, unused to the straight back. The task consisted of writing a letter to a hypothetical provider set in France asking for a refund for a faulty product, to then repeat the exercise in Spanish. As I set out to type the first letter, I noticed the letters on the keyboard were all jumbled up. At home, I had been using an old French laptop for my studies. This was the first time I'd seen a Qwerty keyboard. I stared at it for a moment, hesitant. The woman in the black trousers approached my desk.

"Everything ok? You do speak French, don't you?" she asked, her eyes narrowing.

I took a deep breath and started typing, tentatively at first, then a little faster. After twenty minutes, another woman in pressed grey trousers and high heels collected me.

"The panel is ready for you," she said, her hand guiding me towards a glass fronted door. She unlocked it with a card hanging from the lanyard around her neck. Gesturing towards an empty chair, she invited me to sit, joining two men in black suits and stripy blue shirts on the other side of a large office table. The man I assumed to be the Chair informed me that the interview would last approximately thirty minutes. He seemed friendly, engaging even. I was asked to confirm my name, address, and date of birth.

When I spoke, I denoted a shift in his behaviour. A subtle tension in the shoulders. A raised eyebrow. After three minutes, the chair conferred with his colleagues then turned to me and thanked me for coming.

"We've heard enough," he said, seeing my confusion.

I stood to walk out the way I'd come.

"A word of advice young lady," the Chair said, leaning across the table. "In the future you ought to indicate your nationality on the CV."

I walked out of the building under the watchful eye of the security guard. What had just happened? I wondered. Since I wore my husband's surname, my foreign accent had apparently startled them. I realised they interpreted the omission as a clear sign of my deceitful nature. Just like that, I'd stopped being a valid candidate, and become a dirty liar.

Back at home, I stared at my reflection in the bathroom mirror, wondering what people saw when they looked at me. That evening, I observed the man I had married, sat on that blue sofa we'd purchased together, in the freshly white painted lounge of the Cardiff Bay flat which we called home. He sat in his pyjamas, feet up, watching a rugby game. A beer in one hand and a remote control in the other, he didn't look like a man who could protect anyone. The floor around me dropped for a moment and he became a distant sight. The living room filled with darkness and a weight pressed on my chest. I couldn't breathe. I couldn't … breathe. I stood and walked in the direction of the bathroom, on autopilot. Locking the door behind me, I dropped to the floor and started to sob. What was I doing here? My life was a fraud. I, an impostor.

The next day, walking down Lloyd George Avenue on my way to town, I wondered if in fact some invisible hand had placed me on the proverbial wrong side of the track. Across the avenue was the Cardiff Central to Cardiff Bay line. One stop. Beyond was Butetown, the old Tiger Bay. One of Britain's first multicultural communities where more than fifty nationalities had settled, Somalis rubbing shoulders with Greeks, Yemenis with Italians, all looking for a slice of the Industrial Revolution. There, maybe, I would have belonged.

Paris

The day of my second job interview, the phone rang. I ignored it at first, until the insistence of the dial forced me to reconsider. Looking at the handset, I saw my mother's number and felt wary. It wasn't like her to ring in the middle of the day. We had only exchanged the occasional bitter email since the wedding. Dad's mind had started to slip away shortly after. Thinking he was making a sound investment, he had sunk his life savings in a social housing project in the *banlieues*, leaving my parents penniless. At the bank's request, I was appointed by a judge to oversee a three-year plan to repay the significant overdraft that now hung over their future. My mother had experienced this solution as a betrayal, accusing me of robbing her of all autonomy, whilst she alone fought Dad's mounting incoherence.

The phone clicked as I picked up the receiver in the bedroom. All I could hear at first was silence, then snivels, and sniffles, intercalated with snippets of words.

"Papa ... Cold on the floor ... Locked bathroom door ... Head wound." Then: "He is so cold. He is so cold." Her voice was barely audible.

"I have a job interview, Mum."

"No, you must come. Now." The distress in her voice was shocking.

I didn't make the interview. Instead, I rang the airport and booked the next flight from Cardiff. On the phone, the flight booking woman wouldn't stop talking about her recent holiday in Paris whilst arranging the ticket.

"Treating yourself to a nice trip, love?" she asked, jovial, in a thick Valleys accent.

I remember mumbling something, not quite sure how to reply, not wanting to wound such banal optimism with a display of grief.

"Your poor mum. How is she doing?" Terry asked over the phone when I rang his office next to tell him I was leaving.

"I don't know. I have to go. Need to pack a bag." I snapped, irritated by his question.

Three hours later, I walked out of Charles de Gaulle Airport. Max, my dad's best friend was standing on the concourse, waiting to drive me home. My mother had regained her composure by the time the doorbell rang. She wore a perfectly tailored black dress, a river of pearls, dyed ebony hair à la Jackie O. She let us in, offered to take our coats, directed us to the living room as if we were distant guests.

"You will want to see your father," she told me, in too formal a tone, before I could sit. "The funeral attendants laid him to rest in your bedroom. You know the way," she added.

I moved like an automaton down the familiar corridor. From the door, I could see my father, dressed in a dark suit, resting on the double bed that my parents had been storing for me since Bordeaux. As I approached, I noticed that his face had the shade and consistency of wax, giving him the air of a museum exhibit. I leant forward, pressing my lips against his forehead, feeling for evidence of his passing. What I felt was hard and cold, like a marble statue, a corpse deprived of life. Shaken, I retreated to the living room where my mother was serving orange juice and biscuits. Sat on one of the upright chairs, I listened in silence as she described the logistics of the funeral the following day. When she was done talking, Max excused himself.

"I will go pay my respects now," he said, standing straight as a mast fighting a storm.

He returned a few minutes later, eyes bloodshot and looking lost.

"I'll take my leave now," he said to no one in particular.

My mother rose and walked him to the door.

"Wait. I guess I'll be coming with you Max." I stood up with urgency before he could cross the threshold. "I mean, I'll need to find a hotel," I added, thinking of the corpse laying in my room.

The next day, Max drove me to *Notre Dame de L'Assomption de Passy*, a small community church wedged at the back of a busy retail quarter, in one of the most affluent parts of the city. There, Terry and I had got married less than a year before. Max and I sat in the shadows of the last row. I wanted to disappear, bewildered at the ease with which my mother had slipped from attentive carer into this role of grieving widow. There she was, leading the assembled audience of friends and former colleagues who had flocked back to attend the funeral. She turned and saw us, gesturing for me to come sit by her side. If she felt any resentment towards all those who had vanished, leaving her to battle Dad's mental collapse, she didn't show. They made me sick all those well-wishers bowed, grief-stricken, now that he had had the decency to die. People were absurd, I thought, expunging a profound desire to kick the pew in front of me as the eulogy started.

"Francis trained as a military man ... a career as a ministerial advisor who embodied the ideal of ..." The slow diction. The pauses for effect. A voice used to public speaking. For ten minutes he spewed banalities about my father, in stop motion. An odd choice, I thought. A former colleague, a childhood friend from Morocco. As I sunk into my own thoughts, his voice faded away.

I was never quite sure what Dad did for a living. All my friends had parents with solid professions – lawyers, bankers, surgeons. Dad's career was ephemeral. He had a large office in the centre of Paris, travelled often, never spoke about anything, and always returned with extravagant presents, mementos from foreign lands. Beyond that, I knew not to ask questions, somehow. Before he retired, he had worked at a QUANGO, financing development projects in France's former colonies. I had imagined his to be the role of a saviour for those in need. Yet I couldn't quite square this idea with the armed chauffeur who sometimes collected me from school.

The priest's voice had been replaced by Max's warm baritone, offering me a lift. Back home. To his London flat. "It is no good to be alone," he was saying. Good old Max.

Gagged by grief, we journeyed in silence. Max's fingers clenched at the steering wheel, mirroring the feeling that my ribcage was contracting. As I struggled to control my breath, a violent wailing sound rang into my ears, shattering the silence. Max swerved into the emergency lane, grabbed hold of my shoulders, and held me like you would an armed grenade ready to explode. Pain seared into my flesh. Around us the blurry dark shadow of trees, stripped bare by winter, morphed into monstrous claws, threatening to crush us.

"That's alright," Max replied. "You're going to be alright."

"I wasn't there," I murmured.

Dad's mental collapse had not been gradual. It had started with a single message, left on my answering machine.

"I rang to tell you your mother has been kidnapped. You are not home."

I was on honeymoon with Terry. When I heard the message, I dropped everything, jumped on a plane to Paris. Twelve hours later, I found him quietly sitting in the lounge, waiting. It was the middle of the night.

"Do you know why I'm here Dad?"

"Yes, you are here for your mother's funeral."

"I spoke to Mum, Dad. She is away on a trip," I told him – gently taking hold of his hand – "Mum is fine. Are you ok, Dad?" When I looked at his hand, it struck me how sinewed it was, almost skeletal but for translucent protruding veins that pulsated too hard.

He became agitated. "It is them ... They are trying to confuse me ... They put a magnet in my brain to erase my thoughts."

"Who is 'them', Dad?"

"It was standard practice. The electric treatment. We ... it was all about breaking them. About stripping them of humanity." Dad clutched at my hand. "I see their bloodied bodies on the ochre floor. Limbs missing. Children."

The thought of my father's mysterious trips came to mind.

He tapped his left thumb against each of the left fingers in a repetitive pattern, faster and faster. "I remember. I remember. It is all in there. It is all in here." He tapped at his skull.

"Dad?" I called, "Are you remembering something you witnessed?"

When he looked up it was as if he had seen a ghost.

"You can't see them," he said, eyes searching behind me. "Nobody sees."

Unable to make sense of what he was saying, and frightened to see him look so haunted, I rang SOS psychiatry, asked for a doctor to come. A little man with white hair and red corduroy trousers arrived at the door a few hours later, the distinctive black leather bag of the medical profession by his side.

"I am Doctor Cep, like the mushroom. Do you know why I am here?" he asked my father. Silent, Dad shook his head, no. "I am a doctor in psychiatry. Your daughter here has asked me to come. She is worried about you."

"No, you won't lock me up. I won't let you. I know the law; I know my rights. I will have you arrested." And to me: "It is them."

The little doctor with the red trousers looked a little uncertain. Dad was very convincing in his certitude. "Can I talk to you?" We moved into the lobby.

"Are you sure you want to have him sectioned?" he asked me. "He is rather harmless at present."

"He needs help, something is badly wrong. This morning he thought my mother was dead, now he is talking about torture and seeing ghosts." I was desperate to have him fixed. The little doctor signed the letter authorising an involuntary commitment for a period of twelve days at Sainte Anne mental health hospital. "To assess and stabilise," he said. Under 'diagnosis' I read: 'suspected psychotic episode'.

Cardiff

After I returned to Cardiff, all I felt was an enormous pain crushing my chest. Each day, breathing seemed to require further effort. I would sit and stare at invisible ghosts, incapable of giving Terry the sort of love he expected. I wanted to run away. I needed to run away. He kept insisting that it was grief. That it was normal. That it would get easier, in time. That he was there for me. That I should talk to someone. All I wanted was to stamp the pain out. To not feel. Incapable of keeping up the pretence, Terry's touch on me became unbearable. He loved me too much. Something in me was deeply broken, and I knew even he could not fix it. I started going out more. Staying out late. I picked up men in bars. Made a show of it. If I disgusted him, I reasoned, he would have to let me go.

A year to the day after we got married, he finally called it quits. I moved out with a few things. Found shared accommodation with itinerant workers in Splott. I didn't care anymore what happened to me. For a while, I went through the motions. Each day, I sent CV after CV, looking for work, looking for work, looking for work, never finding any. Each rejection pushing me a little deeper into darkness. I tried office jobs first, then library, retail, waitressing, leafletting cars, but everyone could see I wasn't right. Until, finally, the money ran out, until I defaulted on the rent, until all I had left fitted in a single bag I carried on my back at night. Waiting for the van on Charles Street to drive up with warm food. Waiting for daylight to find a safe spot to sleep. I was terrified someone would steal my shoes whilst I slept, a trick of the mind I knew prevented me from thinking about a worse fate. I wouldn't allow myself to go there. To imagine what else could happen to me on the streets. I had a little tent with me. I told myself it was like camping. I found a spot in Bute Park, a cove by the river Taff, away from the main paths. I pretended I was on holiday, and for a while, during the summer months, I almost believed it too. Except, the disapproving whispers from the odd family passing on the other bank rang loud in my head. Then, after a while, it was as if I wasn't there anymore. People I passed in the street stopped making eye contact, as if I'd become a ghost. As if they could no longer see me.

When days started to get colder, I panicked, thinking soon someone would find me dead in the tent. I had walked past the Housing Advice Centre on St Mary Street a few times. I'd lost count of how long I'd been sleeping rough when I decided to go in. Long enough that I could no longer smell myself.

"You haven't been in the UK long enough to be entitled to any support," a white man with long dreadlocks advised me. The years as a student did not count.

"Unless you find work, you'll have to go back," he added. *Free movement of workers, man.*

I couldn't go back. I thought about my father, lying on his death bed. About the person he had been, and the secrets that had driven him mad. The advisor kept asking more questions. There had been a husband, yes. I wasn't sure where he was now. All I knew was that autumn was coming, nights were getting longer, the food scarcer, my prospects more frightening. Come back tomorrow, he had told me.

I went to step out of the little shopfront squeezed between two nightclubs. Directly in front of me stood a man with short-back-and-sides and a pair of toe-capped boots, barring my route. I had seen him before, pushing around the druggies at the train station. He was arguing with an elderly woman with long, wiry, grey hair. She reminded me of a calm body of water.

"Give me back my girl," he shouted, spit landing on my face.

"I already told you sir; you can't stay here."

Accelerating my pace, I tried to move past them, eyes fixed to the floor. As I did, I noticed the toecaps stepping towards the woman, towards me. I saw the way he clenched his fists and froze. If the toecaps took another step, I would be stamped out of existence like a spider.

"Is there a problem, man?" The voice of the advisor with the white dreadlocks rang, passing me as if I were invisible. I saw his colourful trainers planted next to the woman's sturdy boots. Together, they formed a peculiar barrier between the angry pimp and the door.

"Cops are on their way mate. Better move on," Colourful Trainers added.

They stood, motionless. Colourful Trainers, Walking Boots, Toecaps, me in the middle. In the end, Toecaps turned in the direction of the jungle of homeless people camped outside the train station, his territory. I let out a slow, tentative, trickle of air as he stomped away.

The elderly woman placed her hand on my shoulder, sending a shiver echoing down my spine. She searched my face. "Are you ok, love?"

I nodded, noticing the Women's Aid badge on her t-shirt mirroring a sign above the door. A shared door.

"We help each other out," the dreadlocked man commented with a grin.

A few minutes later, I was scurrying the length of St Mary Street, left past the stone-carved animals perched on the castle wall. I clocked the bear, staring me down as I reached the bridge with his single beady eye. For a second, I could have sworn he was looking right at me. The image of my grandmother and her pet bear flashed in front of my eyes. Arthur. I wished he would come to take me away.

A loud noise pulled me back, a car horn, maybe, and I retreated into Bute Park. Behind me was the stadium, and to my left, Cathedral Road, and the B&B where I had slept a lifetime ago. The bridge over the Taff traced a border from that past. Water. The elderly woman. My mind was full of water. Moving away from the ornamental garden and its rows of benches, I continued along the walled nursery skirted with thick wild vegetation where the park rangers kept their equipment. Where the path forked into densely growing trees, I picked up pace, advancing in a straight line now, as if on autopilot, reaching a clearing by the river, a narrow rocky beach hidden from view. There, I exhaled at the sight of the familiar bag containing my one-person tent, barely visible under a pile of rocks. I retrieved it, unpacked, and pitched the tent, searching for the opening with crazed fingers. Unrolling my sleeping bag, I pushed the rest of my belongings inside the little yellow and blue cavity, dived in, and zipped the world away.

In the night, I awoke to the rushing sound of choppy water beating the fabric walls around me. The floor of the tent undulated as if it were liquid. It had started to rain heavily in the night. The Taff was in full flood. My tent being carried away, like a makeshift raft. Taking in water from all sides. Blind in the darkness, I gathered my belongings like so many buoyancy aids that failed to keep me afloat. Searching for the seam of the zip, I pulled at the small metal clasp, cold water pouring in, threatening to submerge the tent, to drown me. This is it, I thought. I heard a tearing sound, then my ears filled with water and the world went quiet.

Daylight peered through my eyelids, forcing me to shield my face. My limbs ached, from being battered by the riverbed I thought. I no longer felt cold. In fact, I felt a comforting warmth all around me, like the woolly blanket my grandmother used to wrap around me when I was small. I extended a free hand and patted the air. Fur, heaving fur, warm-blooded. I recoiled, standing upright, scanning the space around me for danger. I blinked; certain my mind had betrayed me. Maybe I had hit my head? Maybe I had died after all? In front of me lay a full-sized bear, curled up in the manner of a domesticated pet, paws tucked in, gently purring. As absurd as the thought might be, the animal looked familiar.

"Arthur?" I called.

The bear's ears twitched, his head rising, eyes levelled with my own. I placed a trembling hand on the animal's snout, a little voice in my head telling me I ought to be frightened. Instead, I felt at home. The bear cradled me in his large paws, and I sank into the warmth of his chest. "Arthur," I said again.

5. FRAGMENTS

Whitchurch Mental Health Hospital – Cardiff

I woke to the rough touch of stiff bedding and a sickening smell of disinfectant. Opening my eyes, I blinked a couple of times, trying to make sense of who I was. Arthur and the riverbank had vanished. Around me were four walls the colour of sterile indifference; a single-pane window with frosted glass and no handle; a door, equipped with a keypad lock. It hurt to gather my thoughts. I remembered coming loose from my floating coffin, the icy feel of the river water and the sharp stab of something in the darkness, a rock or maybe a branch. I wasn't dead. My head was throbbing too much, and there was that awful smell.

I heard footsteps, jangling, and a clicking noise. I wondered who would come through the door: a prison guard or a doctor. A woman in white scrubs, carrying a blue paper cup on a brown plastic tray walked in. Her hair was cut short like a man. A little watch was pinned to her immaculate tunic. On her face, I read benevolent concern.

"Hello sweetheart. Good to see you're finally awake," she said without breaking step.

"Where'm I?" I asked.

"Whitchurch Hospital. The police brought you in two nights ago. Said they pulled you out of the Taff." She pointed at a bandage the length of my arm. "Thought you might have been a jumper."

"Was ... was there someone else?"

"Not sure. Can you tell me your name?"

"I ... I'm not sure." I searched my hazy memory. "I don't know."

I felt a weight on my chest, as if a brick had been sewn to my solar plexus.

"That's ok, sweetheart. The doctor will be along soon. Take those." She pointed at the little cup. "They'll help you relax."

I took the plastic tumbler she handed me from the bedside table and downed the two pills at the bottom of the cup.

"Good girl," she said. "Now get some rest."

As she said it, I felt the mass of my eyelids, like curtains weighted down with sewn in pieces of lead. My body softened, relaxing under a comforting warmth.

When I opened my eyes next, I was back on the sunny beach with Arthur.

"How did you get here?" His voice echoed inside my head.

Memory came to me in fragments, like scraps of paper that had come detached from an unravelling notebook. I turned them upside down, placed them on the floor, trying to find a thread I could follow. Lost. I had lost something. I stared at the bear, feeling the sun warming my face. "Where *is* here, Arthur?"

The nurse led me down the corridor towards a brightly lit dayroom populated with interchangeable grey figures in discordant pyjama sets and threadbare slippers. She pointed at a table on which stacks of cardboard boxes with missing flaps were piled like a disorderly Jenga.

"Feel free to play," the nurse said, inviting me to sit.

"*Jeux de société*," I replied.

"What's that?"

"Board games. In French they're called society's games, or high society's games maybe, I'm not sure. My grandmother played a lot of board games."

"So, you're French then? That's a start. In any case, the doctor will be seeing you shortly."

I watched the stout woman walk away then moved towards the window, hoping for some fresh air. On closer inspection, I realised the handle had been removed. Letting out a deep sigh, I redirected myself towards a heavily padded chair basked in sunlight, with a high back. I immediately liked it. It masked the other occupants from view. My very own island.

"You said you'd lost something?" I heard as an echo.

"Sorry?" I replied, looking around.

At my feet, Arthur was curled up in the afternoon sunshine. He lifted his muzzle in my direction. "You said you'd lost something."

"I ... I thought I knew ..."

Sainte Anne Mental Health Hospital – Paris

Marianne arrived three hours after her husband was admitted to the psychiatric ward at Sainte Anne. Walking to the reception desk, she asked to speak to the doctor. Instead, the nurse handed her a leaflet. "Read this first." It described the internment procedure with a colourful infographic. *GUIDANCE REQUIRES THAT THE PATIENT BE SEEN WITHIN AN HOUR OF ARRIVAL* it read.

"And has he been seen yet?"

"No, not yet I'm afraid."

"That's not what it says should happen," Marianne replied, waving the leaflet. "I want to speak to someone."

"Understand Ma'am, it's the bank holiday."

"Right. What are you saying?"

"Well, the administration decreed that all assessments must be carried out by two psychiatrists, assisted by a mental health nurse."

"And?"

"And, we don't have two psychiatrists on staff today ... or tomorrow for that matter."

"Can't you get someone to assess him? I'll sign a waiver."

"We can't do that. Sorry."

"So, you're saying that he is being detained, but you're not going to provide care? That's barbaric."

"Well, it says here that the attending nurse has administered antipsychotic to stabilise your husband's mood."

"But you don't know what's wrong with him? I want to take him home. Go get him please."

"I'm afraid you'll have to get permission from the police prefect. In any case, your husband cannot be released until he has been seen by a doctor who can confirm a diagnosis."

"And you're telling me there is nobody to issue a diagnosis? This is absurd." Marianne walked out of the hospital and into the car park where she found her daughter. "What did you do?" she said, throwing her arms in the air.

On day twelve, when he was finally discharged, Marianne collected her husband from the waiting room. She found him sat, motionless, a plastic bag containing his neatly folded possessions on his lap. He had been diagnosed with *reactive psychosis*. The psychiatrist commented that the patient displayed signs of trauma the likes of which had been widely documented in the 1960s with victims and perpetrators of torture during the Algerian War. The radiologist noted that a CT scan had revealed an inconclusive shadow on his brain. He asked Marianne whether there was anything in her husband's past which could explain this type of trauma. She met the question with a shrug, her eyes drifting towards the barred window.

"The best thing is to keep him sedated. Give him two of these each day," the doctor concluded, handing Marianne a prescription sheet. A chemical straitjacket, Marianne thought, deflated, as she exited the room. They had no idea what was wrong with him.

Whitchurch Mental Health Hospital – Cardiff

The monotony of life in the hospital soon became my new normal. Devoid of surprises. Comforting. The day was broken only by the visit of a hospital nurse pushing a stainless-steel cart into the day room, twice daily, morning and night. For an instant, her presence seemed to bring order to the chaos of the patients' lounge. Over time, my memory seemed to return. In dribs at first, images mostly. Familiar sensations. Smells. Moments of clarity interspersed with sudden anguish and confusion, mitigated by the antipsychotic drugs.

I lined up amongst the others, ready to be handed my little paper cup, filled with colourful pills. Then the nurse wheeled the cart away, and we dispersed again. I retreated towards the space I had claimed as my own. Arthur joined me and we basked in the sunlight, safe from the heavy rain that poured beyond the hospital barred window.

"What made you stay?" Arthur asked. "You had plans after the Erasmus year."

"I thought I was following in my mother's footsteps."

"So, what happened?"

"Nothing was as I thought."

Paris

Marianne joined the queue at the *Mairie* of the 16th arrondissement with a copy of Francis's death certificate. She had come to renew her passport. They used to joke that between them, they had covered every continent apart from Antarctica. Marianne would smile, adding that there was still time.

"Next," the civil servant called through the Tannoy, a sign flashing above booth number 14. "Renewal?" he inquired in a voice that reminded her of an automaton.

Marianne nodded.

"Papers."

She handed the wiry man the required documents: proof of his passing, her birth certificate, and the blue *livret de famille* Francis had once handed her on *autopista 90* and which now contained a record of the birth of their daughter.

"I see," he said, looking over the final piece. "And did you bring your certificate of naturalisation?"

"I beg your pardon?"

"It states here on your birth certificate that you were born in Morocco. Did you bring the document confirming when you acquired the French nationality?"

Marianne gave the man a bemused look at first, waiting for him to crack a smile, as if his request was a joke in poor taste.

"I don't have all day. Do you have all the documentation or not?"

"I have my existing French passport," she replied, pulling it out of her handbag with an exaggerated sense of triumph.

"That's not enough," the civil servant replied, not taking the time to open the expired passport. "Do you have your naturalisation paper or not?"

"No, of course not."

"In that case you will need to make another appointment and bring the correct documentation." He kept putting an emphasis on that last word, documentation.

"But it is absurd. I'm French, for Christ's sake. I have been all my life."

"Not according to these papers," the man replied, separating each syllable as if speaking to a simpleton.

At this, Marianne lost all sense of decorum and threw her bag to the floor, gesticulating in the man's direction, feeling her face burning red, "This is insane," she shouted at him. "Don't you know your own history, young man?"

Unfazed, the man sighed. "Look Ma'am, if you are not happy with the process, you can fill a complaint form in triplicate and send it to the head office. In the meantime, I am going to ask you to leave."

Marianne froze for a moment, gathering her thoughts. This couldn't be happening. She took another look at the petty civil servant, noticing his greasy forehead for the first time. The sort of man who took pleasure in using his limited authority as a 'screw you' to the upper bourgeoisie of the area, she thought. Yet she denoted something else in his attitude. The disdain with which he had spoken to her. She dismissed the idea of requesting to speak to his superior. Something told her it would only make matters worse. Instead, she picked up the discarded handbag, and left the civic office, holding her back as straight as her age would allow, grumbling under her breath.

Outside, she collapsed on a green Art Deco bench surrounded by pigeons and searched her address book. This would require a different approach. She found the contact she was looking for and punched the number in her mobile phone with her index finger.

"Maître Goitron," she asked the receptionist.

When the family notary answered, she released a torrent of invectives about the ineptitude of the French civil service without taking a single breath. Once he sensed the flow of her outrage was diminishing, Goitron asked a few questions, waiting out the animated torrent of answers.

"Yes, I see," he finally concluded. "I've seen this before. The

Government has become so obsessed with immigration that common sense and historical context have been thrown out the window."

"Right," Marianne replied, as if the notary had confirmed a diagnosis of insanity. "How do we fix this?"

Maître Goitron explained that Marianne would need to obtain copies of her parents' birth certificates to demonstrate a link to France.

"But Maître, it won't help. My mother was born in Indochina and my father in India."

"What about your grandparents?"

"India, both of them. The generation before is from a small village in the Gers region."

"Then we will have to go back to them, I'm afraid."

Goitron put together a small dossier tracking the genealogy of Marianne's family since they had first left French soil, some hundred and fifty years before. Some had travelled to Réunion Island and established themselves there. The bulk of the family had moved to Pondicherry when it first became a trade outpost, including a grandmother who had subsequently followed her husband to Indochina.

"Is your daughter Charlotte the only family member born in France?" Goitron asked when he met Marianne to present his findings to her.

"That's correct," Marianne replied. "She expatriated to the United Kingdom, however."

"Man's incredible capacity for adaptation," Goitron commented, half to himself.

"Woman."

"I beg your pardon?"

"Woman's capacity for adaptation," Marianne corrected.

"Quite," Goitron replied.

Whitchurch Mental Health Hospital

I lost count of how many days I sat in the high-backed chair with Arthur for sole companion. "Everything I thought I left behind is no more," I told him. "Bonne-Maman died when I was at university. Dad after I moved here. Uncle Jean, whom I didn't even really know. Did I tell you that he had already been buried when we heard from the nuns running the hospice?" I sighed. "That's my fate. To die alone, away from any familiar face."

Arthur rumbled, nuzzling the palm of my hand.

"I wanted an adventure. Like yours, with Bonne-Maman. Hopping from cloud to cloud, without a care in the world."

Arthur pressed his warm body against my leg.

"You're right. It is a self-imposed exile. But if this life in the UK is not the right one, then who am I, Arthur? Where do I belong?"

Warm tears filled my eyes, blurring the image of the faithful bear.

"I ... I went looking for ... for something that wasn't there." I coughed. "An elusive freedom ... that never existed." I pulled on the collar of my dressing gown. "I feel ... soluble." I wiped a heavy stream of snot with the sleeve of my dressing gown, pressing my lids shut to arrest the flow of tears. When I opened my eyes, a man with gold-rimmed glasses and an orange bowtie had materialised in place of Arthur. He smiled at me.

"You've been carrying a lot of broken pieces. A lot of grief," he told me. "It is time to come out the other side."

I'll never know why I saw Arthur in those days. Maybe he was the closest image to family I could conjure up at a distance. The only one who could materialise at will and fill the gap all those deaths had left behind. After he vanished, the jovial doctor prescribed a long course of talking therapy.

"You suffered an acute psychotic episode," he explained. "Are you prepared to say a little about what brought it on?"

"I don't know," I told him. Ignorance always the best defence.

Changing tack, he urged me to address what he called my *precarious circumstances*. He put me in touch with a charity that offered emergency accommodation. I was moved to the outpatient ward and attended therapy sessions three times a week for a year. In those sessions, I was taught the importance of naming the thoughts that burdened me. The guilt I experienced for having had my father sectioned. The grief from losing him a second time. The anger at all that silence around my uncle's exile. My own sense of dislocation.

London

Immediately after the funeral, Max invited me to stay with him at his London flat on Cavendish Street. From his sofa, I stared through the window at the plague of pigeons colonising the rooftops for two solid days. On the third, he presented me with a plate of spaghetti and a glass of port, his way to pull me out of the daze, I suppose. "Good for the soul," he said. "Grief has its own schedule you know. Give it time. What happened to your dad wasn't your fault."

"You don't understand, Max. After the hospital, Dad never made eye contact again. He became ... hollow. I mean ... he took the pills for a few days."

"Until he stopped?"

"Yes. Mum said she had to crush them into his food. For his own good, she said. No doubt she was worried about what people thought."

"You know that's not fair."

"Maybe. He spoke of conspiracies, of theft, of land taken and people brutalised. In the end, you were the only friend who stood by him. You and Mum." I sighed loudly. "What really happened to Dad?" I asked.

Max looked at me with a strange expression. "There isn't an explanation for all things," he said.

"I just wish someone would explain this." I remembered something then. "Max, did you know Mum was married before Dad?"

Whitchurch Mental Health Hospital

At our first counselling session, the talking therapist asked why I had left Paris. I gave her the same generic story I had given everyone else. A boy.

"Do you mean your first husband?"

I shrugged.

"Do you mean someone before? In Paris?"

My body collected into a ball, knees folding into my chest. "The City of Love," I whispered.

She considered me for a while. "That's not how you see it?"

What was Paris for me? Now there was a good question. Not the place of tourist attractions, that was for certain. My parents' apartment, school, the park where I played with my friends, church on Sundays. An enclosed community, delineated by four pillars, steeped in an illusion of safety. I grew up under the watchful eye of involved neighbours and benevolent shopkeepers, warned against the dangers that loomed beyond those boundaries.

Paris

On Saturdays my parents and I travelled *Rive Gauche*, to the Latin Quarter. My father drove whilst I sat at the back, watching through the window as we crossed the bridge over the river Seine from our neighbourhood on the *Rive Droite*. The land on the other side was strange, filled with cafés, clubs, and cinemas where artists, intellectuals and students rubbed shoulders with global hordes of wealthy tourists seeking the experience described in countless novels. A place of *de-paysement*, disorientation. A place curated by my father who had lived in this part of Paris as a student. He would select the *terrace de café* for our lunch, the film we would view. For two hours, we would sit in one of the dark projection rooms marking the *Place de L'Odéon*. My father abhorred French films. He always treated them as alien, deploring their heavy humour, tortured storylines, and verbose dialogues. He preferred the Manichean simplicity of Hollywood movies, with subtitles. Their ability to transport. To make you dream. Afterwards, he would drive us home, back to our neighbourhood on the right bank of the river. Maybe in my childish mind, the adventures actors played out on screen merged into the storyboard of my own parents' life.

At sixteen, I moved to another school, further away, in another neighbourhood. I would need to take the metro. My mother reminded me to guard against strangers, people 'not from our world'. The message was clear. Beware of men, just like the one who sat opposite me one day. He stood out, awkwardly wrapped in a large beige trench coat, his body jolted by recurring twitches. Intrigued by the movement, I made eye contact, which he apparently took as an invitation to reveal himself, unzipped, flaccid. My back stiffened. My eyes scattered, caught for an instant by the rhythmic movement of his hand, up and down, up and down. As my eyes brushed past his face, looking for a safer focal point, I noticed how the release tamed the twitch that had distorted him a moment before. Satisfied, he closed his coat, and I anchored my gaze on the foldaway seat next to him. The two of us remained, immobile, until the next station. When the metro doors rang open, he stood and evaporated amongst the morning commuters. "Creep," a school friend commented when I relayed the experience. "But don't you know better than to make eye contact?"

Whitchurch Mental Health Hospital

"How did that make you feel?" the therapist asked.

"I don't know ... There was a certain acceptance of those things ... back then."

"I mean, your friend's judgement."

"I'm not sure what you mean by that."

"Your friend's reaction. Somehow, she shifted the blame on to you, suggested you, your behaviour had elicited that man's reaction."

"I did look."

"Charlotte, you were a child. Victim of sexual harassment."

"Oh, I wouldn't call it that."

The doctor frowned.

"And Wales? Why did you come?" she asked another time.

"In Wales I could become independent from my parents. I wanted to stand on my own two feet."

"Could you not have done that in France?"

"When I turned sixteen, my mother decided to go back to work. He hated the idea, my father. Kept saying she didn't need to work ... That he could provide ... As if her wanting a job was an affront to him. I think in his mind, her role was to host dinner parties, to support him. It never occurred to him that she might want other things. Painting was ok because he saw it as a hobby, but an office job ..." I laughed an uneasy laugh.

"You mentioned your father was ambiguous about women in his own work."

"Yes. He described all the secretaries as harpies. The worst was a businesswoman he often had dealings with. Mrs Dominges, I think was her name. She smoked a cigar in board meetings. That infuriated him."

"Why do you think that is?"

"I don't know. Maybe because he thought her taking a job questioned his status as provider?"

"That makes sense. And what happened with your mother?"

"She is strong-headed. Went back to work anyway."

"And what did you think about all that?"

"I think ... I think that's what drew a wedge between us, my mother and me. I ... felt compelled to side with him, demonstrate my loyalty."

"And your mother?"

"I was incredibly proud of her for going back to work like that. I don't think I ever told her, but it had a profound effect on me. There she was, standing on her own two feet even though financially she didn't have to. She was formidable."

"So, coming to Wales ... you were not so much seeking your father's approval as your mother's? Following in her footsteps?"

"I suppose. The travel. It was hers. I mean ... he was away for work all the time, but it was her movement that was significant to me. Meaningful, you know?"

"How so?"

"Because, even then, I realised society didn't recognise women like her, I suppose. Women who made decisions for themselves, travelled on their own, refused to be a man's sidekick. I'd grown up reading travel adventures written by men. Nobody wrote stories like that about women."

"So, in moving to Wales, you were trying to emulate the women in your family?"

"Yes. No. It's more complicated. I moved to escape. Not going *to* Wales, so much. Running away *from* Paris."

"Can you tell me why?"

Paris

I had just turned seventeen the first time a boy asked me out. We lived on the same street. Went to the same school. A few years older, his parents had installed him in his own flat, one of those student rooms on the top floor of their building. It gave him an aura of maturity.

"Come over, I'll show you my place," he'd said, walking me back from school one day.

His room was about the size of my mother's bathroom. It had its own sink. A space with large cushions spread out on the floor, moonlighting as a living room. A bed built into a sort of alcove.

He handed me a platter of grapes and blue cheese. "You must eat those with wine. It brings out the flavour," he said, presenting me with a plastic tumbler, filled to the rim with red. Despite the shabby decor, it felt sophisticated. We were playing grown up. I was nervous, so I drank. Too much. Too fast. When the room started to vacillate, I realised my mistake. I stood up, thanked him for his hospitality.

"I'd better go home," I told him with a smile.

He watched as I swayed towards the door, rattled at the handle, failed to open the door.

"A little help?" I said.

He took a step towards me, paused, as if suspended in mid-air, then diverted towards the bed.

"Come sit next to me a minute," he said, tapping the cover next to him. I noticed the wine had stained his lips purple, giving his face the air of a grotesque mask.

"I want to go," I insisted.

"Just a minute," he repeated, cocking his head to one side.

Only for a minute, I told myself. As soon as I sat, he wove his fingers into my hair, tilting my head, not gently like in the films, but forcefully, bringing his face directly above mine. I opened my mouth to speak, and he stuck his tongue down my throat. I tried to move my head left and right, but he pulled at my hair, yanked me flat onto my back. I felt a searching hand fumble with the metal buckle of his

136

belt, pushing up my pleated skirt, pulling at my cotton underwear. I felt the weight of his body as he lay on top of me, making it hard to grasp for air. I felt the pain deep inside me. No, I thought. No. But no sound came out. I stopped struggling. Lay motionless on the sheets. It'll only take a minute, I told myself. I searched an invisible point on the opposite wall, willing my mind away from my body. I saw, as if from above, his white buttocks pounding and pounding and pounding. Then he jerked, groaned, went still. After another minute he stood. Fixed his clothes. Stepped away from the bed and pulled a key out of his back pocket.

"You can go now," he said, unlocking the door.

I rose, uncertain, pocketed my pants, straightened my skirt, and stepped through the door, running down the stairs for fear he would change his mind. In the street, the cold February air hit me like a slap. It was dark outside. I kept running until I reached my parents' building, wanting to scream for someone to help me. But then I stopped. I stood on the other side of the road, holding on to a parking meter, catching up with my thoughts. In that moment I considered all the lives that I would never live. A respectable husband. A loving family. A fulfilling social life. So many doors. Closed. The weight of his body was in me, marking me, a stain that I thought would never go away. I knew. I knew what people would say. That I had asked for it. I crossed the road after a while, let myself into the apartment. It was dark. My parents were asleep. In my room, I got undressed, placed the clothes into the washing basket, took a shower.

I remember feeling grateful a few weeks later when my period came. Beyond that, my body was no longer my own. The weight of his body. The smell of alcohol on his breath. The sound of skin rubbing against skin resonating in my ears. These things, I carried inside everywhere. The event itself, I pushed away from my mind, willed it to disappear. Where I had stood before, there was only rage. Silent rage. I stopped writing in my diary, then. Shocked with anger and shame, I could no longer find the words.

Whitchurch Mental Health Hospital

"You internalised a huge trauma," the therapist said.

"It was my fault for being so stupid."

"What gives you that idea?"

"Most of my father's work colleagues had mistresses. They paraded them at dinner parties, whilst the wives stayed home to mind the children. It is called 'having an adventure' in French. Bizarre, isn't it? As if those women were exotic destinations."

"How did you feel about that?"

"I used to laugh at the sexist jokes, you know. As if they couldn't touch me. It was almost schizophrenic. There were two types of women. The respectable marrying type who stayed at home, and the others. That day, I forever joined the rank of those women my father despised."

"Do you think what happened affected your relationship with your parents?"

"I don't know. I suppose they'd sold me this idea that people in our world were somehow morally superior. Respectable. Trustworthy."

"You felt betrayed?"

"I guess ... thinking about it now ... I can see why you'd say that."

"How would you say it?"

"After that night I felt like I was walking around the neighbourhood with a placard on my back saying *damaged goods*, you know what I mean?"

The therapist nodded, then leant softly towards me. "What happened, it happened to you, Charlotte. Not because of something you did. Because of someone else's perception of women as objects."

"I don't know."

"It is common for victims of sexual violence to take on the blame, because of the way society frames the position of women. But Charlotte, you were the victim here. You are the victim, still."

"It was a long time ago. Water under the bridge and all that," I sniggered.

"Is that what you've been doing?"

"What do you mean?"

"Pretending it didn't happen."

"No point lingering."

"And how is that working for you?" she gestured at the room around us.

"Not so good, I guess. The thing is, even now I couldn't speak about what happened with my parents."

"That's alright. You can talk to me. Tell me how you feel."

"I ... I know, in my head, that I was just a child. Doesn't help though."

"Why do you say that?"

"The damage is done. It is ingrained in me, like a crack."

"What do you mean?"

"I suppose, you're taught to see the world a certain way. And then something like that happens, and suddenly everything you thought you knew shatters. That sort of thing will split you down the middle. There is no going back. You can't un-know the things you've learnt."

"It takes a long time to overcome such a trauma, but believe me, it can be done."

"Do you think that's why my marriage broke down? Because I'm all broken inside?"

"Is that what you think?"

I thought about our discussion. Was that why I'd really come to Wales? To hide from the pain? It was easier to ignore what had happened because everything was different here ... but then I'd gone and got married.

"I realise now that I only married Terry because I saw him as a sort of protector."

"How was your relationship?"

"Do you mean ... I went through the motions. Did what was expected."

"Did you enjoy any of it?"

"My body … It is like, it isn't really mine. Not really … real. It doesn't matter what happens to it, you know."

"It is called dissociative trauma. It is a symptom of post-traumatic stress disorder. That's how your brain has learnt to cope with triggers in the absence of treatment. I can help you."

"How did you feel when your father passed?" she asked another day.

"Something broke inside my soul. I no longer cared about anything. All those things that had seemed important, that made me look … normal. A husband. A career. It all felt hollow."

"Is it possible your father's death gave you permission to feel, rather? To experience the trauma you'd repressed for fear of his judgement? Permission to be yourself?"

"Maybe. Except, I didn't know who that was. I … I had an image of who I was, part of this big migrating tribe …"

"Yes?"

"In France there is this idea that anyone can assimilate, become part of this vision of universal France my parents carted around like a badge of honour. When I came to Wales, I tried hard to assimilate. I stayed away from French people. Learnt the mores here with the diligence of an ethnologist. I suppose I thought assimilation would whitewash the past. Offer me a fresh start."

"And …"

"And the more I tried, the more I felt people were reducing me to this series of labels. French. White – Other. Always outside. Always pushed back. Damaged goods."

"How did that make you feel?"

"I unravelled, as if someone had pulled on a string and all the pieces that had held me together came undone at once."

"Why do you think you hallucinated Arthur?" she asked.

"I'm not sure. Maybe I was trying to hold on to the myth. Maybe it was too painful to consider the alternative."

"What is the alternative?"

"I'm not sure."

"Does your family's colonial past bother you?"

"For my ancestors to have benefited from a brutal rule that's completely at odds with everything we learnt at school about the universal values of the Republic, it is hard to comprehend."

"But you're not responsible."

"Maybe not, yet everyone is acting like it was a historic blip, like one of those pinned butterflies in glass trays at the Natural History Museum. But it isn't true, is it?"

"What isn't true?"

"That the past stays in the past."

"No, not in my experience."

"Is there such thing as inherited guilt? How do you say in English? The sins of the father?"

"It's been theorised in other contexts, yes."

"That's how I feel. That by believing the stories of travel they recorded in their notebooks; I somehow condoned the crimes of the past. Perpetuated the silence."

"Do you see yourself returning to France?"

"No. In France, nothing is as it seems. I could never go back. Besides, I realise how imprisoned I felt. Always trying to belong."

"And here?"

"Here I know I don't belong. That I will never belong. It's strangely liberating."

6. NOMADIC

Cardiff

When Max heard I'd been in hospital, he sent a cardboard box taped shut with brown packing tape. With the box was a note. *I hope you find what you are looking for.* Inside were some pictures, a handful of notebooks full of unreadable annotations and mnemonics in my father's writing, some books. Amongst them, annotated in pencil and decorated with a fan of colourful Post-it notes was one entitled *History of the Mafia.* Flicking through it, I noticed the introduction was credited to a distant uncle, Armand, my aunt Elizabeth's husband. I only had a faint memory of the man whose Mediterranean villa we used to visit when I was a child. In my mind, he was tall, commanding, a jovial storyteller. The preface introduced him as the former Head of the SDECE, the Secret Service that had operated in France during the Cold War.

Opening the book to the foreword, I discovered a name in my father's handwriting: Andres. The same name I'd once found engraved on the inside of a wedding ring. The page was marked. A reference to a country-wide manhunt across Brazil in which a man named Andres and his acolytes had been arrested as part of a joint operation between local police and French and American secret services. The Latin Connection, as they were known, were extradited by the CIA for drug smuggling. That certainly explained my mother's reaction that day, with the engraved ring.

Reaching for my laptop, I dropped Andres's full name into a search engine, not really expecting to find any clues after so long. There were no digitalised records going back that far, I told myself. Amongst a list of mostly irrelevant search results, an article from *The New Yorker* dated from the 1970s caught my attention. It reported on the indictment of nineteen drug smugglers and mentioned the Latin Connection. The article listed Andres by name, referring to an Italo-Colombian pilot who had been arrested in Bogotá.

Calling up another search, I added the middle name I had found in the article. Another hit. This time an article published in Portuguese by a Brazilian magazine, promoting a book on the activities of the Cosa Nostra, the Italian mafia, in Brazil. The article was illustrated with a black and white picture, a police line-up. There he was, third from the left, balding and much thicker, but recognisable, the man from the old photograph my mother had shown me when I was twelve, towering over eight shady looking characters. Then, I noticed the date on the article. *It couldn't be.* Looking up the author, I found another Brazilian newspaper about an arrest and some drug activities in Salvador over a fifty-year period. Portuguese was close enough to Spanish that I understood the main points. Andres was suspected of the murder of two police officers in Colombia and of the death of a 16-year-old girl. Everything I had found to this point mentioned him in passing, a cog in a larger operation. This article was different. It was about him. I read on. *Andres acted as the Head of Commerce for the Cosa Nostra, overseeing heroin production destined for the European market, from Salvador, via Brazil.* I shuffled on my seat, uneasy. Something didn't quite add up. I continued. *Recently arrested, he is being accused of links to organised crime, drug trafficking and money laundering.* Bewildered, I stood up, knocking my chair to the floor. It couldn't be. I took a deep breath, reread the sentence. *Recently arrested ... he is ...* Present. I turned around, grabbed the back of the chair, and stood it upward in the middle of the room, dropping back on its seat with all my weight. There had to be a mistake. Andres was dead. My mother had intimated that much.

Slowly, warily, I dragged myself back to the desk. The article went on. Towards the end was a little biography. It confirmed that the man had started his career as a pilot for the Colombian airline, Avianca. To complement his salary, he had taken to trafficking cigarettes, before discovering a more lucrative market with heroin. The picture from my childhood of the man in uniform flashed in front of my eyes. I stared at the blurred picture of the elderly man with unkept hair and a stained blue shirt which illustrated the

146

article. The arrest had taken place only months before. The article mentioned a previous arrest at the US border and an unbelievable story about how Andres had escaped, fleeing across the Canadian border, on foot, walking 50 kilometers in the snow, to Montreal. According to the journalist, he would have obtained a false passport to travel back to Brazil where he was able to disappear.

For several minutes, I just sat, words from the articles jumping in front of my eyes. An email to my mother, typed absentmindedly. A list of questions. How would I explain what I had been doing? I pressed the delete button and watched as each individual letter disappeared from the screen, erasing any evidence of the cacophony that raged inside my head. I looked up the Brazilian journalist. Found an email address.

Dear Sir,

You do not know me. I am carrying out genealogical research about the former wife of a man you mention in your book, Andres D. I found the article you wrote about him and wondered whether you would agree to speak with me, to share what you know about him. I am particularly interested in the period he spent in Colombia in the 1960s. I don't know if you speak English. I speak Spanish and French also if it helps.

Obrigado,
Charlotte

I pressed the send button and waited for the whooshing confirmation the message had been successfully dispatched.

A few minutes later, the computer pinged.

Sure. Happy to talk.

We exchanged numbers. Arranged a call for the following day. Closing the lid of my laptop, I wondered about the time difference between Cardiff and Rio de Janeiro.

Cartagena

After their wedding, Marianne gave up work to focus on the house Andres had purchased for them in the suburbs of Cartagena. With its whitewashed walls, the house reminded Marianne of her childhood. She took it as a positive sign and dived into sashes of colourful fabrics for the sofas; samples of paint for the walls; catalogues of designer furniture, hoping to fashion a perfect existence with her husband. In only a few months, the villa echoed with symbols of the international lifestyle that Marianne had so aspired to. White linen and copper fans marked the three bedrooms upstairs. The large kitchen was tiled in vibrant Moorish blue. The reception room welcomed guests with large alabaster vases heavy with bouquets, the likes of which Marianne had admired at the Raffles hotel in Singapore. The house was her domain, a place where she exerted full control, apart from a small study which Andres had claimed as his own. The one room in the house which always remained locked.

Andres had just returned from a series of Bogotá–Miami flights that night. His eyes were bloodshot from lack of sleep. He dropped his bags on the bed and told Marianne he needed a shower. As he did, Marianne thought to unpack his bag. Scooping the pile of dirty laundry, her hand caught onto something. Lifting away the clothes, she revealed a large wedge of green banknotes. Dollars, she recognised; her eye attracted towards a strange object in the bottom of the bag. She reached to pick it up, peeling off the oil cloth wrapped around it. It was heavy, hard, cold. She had never held a revolver before.

A sound coming from the direction of the bathroom pulled her back into the room. Andres. In one step he was beside her. He swiped the weapon off her hands, gripping the cannon tightly, hitting her with its grip.

"Why are you snooping, *mujer*?" he said.

By the time he stopped, her face had already swollen enough for her left eye to be completely shut. The pain in her chest made her fear a broken rib.

"Look what you made me do," he said, pointing at her face.

This time, Marianne didn't question what she had done to deserve such a beating. Over the three weeks before her full recovery, she thought about her circumstances. The man she had married was clearly not the kind, heroic pilot she had thought him to be, but rather a possessive, short-tempered man prone to violent outbursts. With the gun and the money, the wealthy business partners and their yachts suddenly took on a different texture.

Marianne became weary, acting overly compliant, making sure not to give her husband any cause to lose his temper. Outwardly absorbed in her role as the perfect hostess, she started to pay attention to her husband's business conversations, gleaning here and there that Andres was selling his ability to cross border control, unchecked. There was talk of safe routes, intercepted cargoes, delivery times. The men's mounting greed was evident to her. Soon, it wasn't enough for Andres to smuggle drugs in his pilot's luggage. His business partners wanted more.

Following his advice, they purchased a Mau Mau plane, which he offered to pilot.

"They are small and fast. Ideal to avoid detection," Marianne overheard him tell them.

The more she heard, the more frightened she grew. At least, she told herself, Andres would be away more. The parties were fewer now, or rather Andres no longer brought her along. Alone in the house, she was at the mercy of his mood swings. She couldn't stay there. But where would she go? She couldn't return to Morocco now that the country had claimed its independence. In his letters, Jean always seemed aloof. And her mother, well ... So where? Her other problem was that her husband knew everyone working in the Colombian airspace. Finding safe passage would cost more than she was able to save from her groceries allowance alone. The longer she waited, she reasoned, the greater the risk of Andres noticing the cash going missing. She needed to find work.

Returning to her old job wasn't an option. Andres had been very clear that her role was as his spouse now. That he would not tolerate her working. She would have to find something around his absences, which were erratic.

Walking to the market one day, she noticed that some of the stallholders were buying bulk stock from local amateur suppliers. She fell into conversation with a toothless Indian lady in traditional dress who was selling wooden lamps carved, she said, by her grandson. A large incandescent light bulb perched on the stall. Pressed by Marianne, the ancient woman explained that the stand holder took a cut to sell the products and cover their market stand fee, the supplier kept the rest. Marianne nodded and thanked the woman.

The same afternoon, she went to the local library and found a book about lampshade making. She sat in the moist heat of the poorly lit library, absorbed in her reading. The next day, she returned to the market, bought a length of silk fabric, some paper, a box of metal rings, and some fabric glue. The house was empty when she returned. She dropped the materials on the kitchen counter and proceeded to craft a lampshade. The first attempt was very unstable, and when she tried it on a lamp in the lounge, it hung sideways against the lightbulb, blackening the paper until eventually it caught fire. Undeterred, Marianne opened the windows, fanned the room, and returned to the kitchen to craft another. This time, the finished product was firmer, but the excess glue leaked onto the delicate silk fabric, making a large stain, shaped like a fried egg.

By nightfall, she had produced five lampshades, all equally unsatisfactory. She was tired and her fingers, thick with glue, ached from bending the metal components into shape. Yet, in a few hours, she had learnt to use the blade of her hand to flatten the fabric onto the paper, wiping with a cloth to avoid any excess glue from spoiling the silk. She raised her sixth creation to the kitchen light and felt a sense of deep satisfaction. Not bad, she thought. She took the lampshade to the lounge and screwed it onto the lamp. It remained perfectly balanced, without touching the lightbulb. She flicked the switch, and the pale blue silk softened the incandescent light into a pleasant glow. She switched off the light, packed all her materials into a box which she hid in the wardrobe amongst her old uniform, washed the glue off each finger with attention, then slid into bed.

Marianne used money she had saved from her food allowance to buy more material, creating a range of colourful shades to dress the carved wooden lamps. Over the weeks, she became more adventurous, adding fringes, inspired by memories of her childhood home. The old lady, pleased with the arrangement which had greatly enhanced her own stock, paid Marianne generously. After a few weeks, she had amassed a fair amount, but not enough. At this rate, it would take her years. The wedge of dollars from Andres's contraband flashed in her mind. He had to keep it somewhere in his office.

The escape route itself had come to her whilst she was sitting in her kitchen making yellow lampshades, overlooking the ballet of shipping containers, heading to and from Cartagena harbour. With the high traffic of boats in the area, she reasoned that she could pay someone to conceal her in one of the shipping-containers. The dockers always stopped to wave at her when she went to the port to buy fresh fish. Maybe she could negotiate a place on a ship. She would need a weapon.

The next morning, she walked to the seafront, determined. She asked around, until a fisherman pointed to an office, deep inside the docks. The building was container-shaped, with a sign on the door that read *Dock Master*. For a moment, she hesitated. Inside the rectangular box was a fierce-looking man with short jet-black hair and a shirt that revealed a muscular build. He sat behind an office desk, looking out of place amongst the piles of what she guessed were shipping manifestos.

151

"I hear you are looking for a ship to Europe, little lady," he said, in an accent that seemed both familiar and alien. "Won't your husband be missing you?" he added, pointing at the ring on her finger. The smirk pulling at the corner of his mouth brought bile to the back of Marianne's teeth. Now wasn't the time to show weak will. She took a deep breath, steadied herself, and replied, "It is my husband I am hoping to join, Señor. He works abroad. Has fallen ill, and ..."

With one hand he interrupted her. "Fine. Your business is yours, as long as the money is right."

She took another deep breath, surprised at the ease with which she had lied.

"How much do you have?" the man asked.

She opened her purse and showed him the pile of dollars.

"Alright," he said, "Come back tomorrow. Bring the cash."

She thanked him, turned around and walked back.

At the house, she packed a bag with a change of clothes, her passport, a book, and her husband's gun wrapped in a towel. "Just in case," she told herself out loud. Marianne soaked herself in the bath for a long time, washing away the dirt she had felt in the presence of the dock master. Andres wasn't due back for another couple of days. She would have a decent head start. Standing in front of the mirror, she cut off her long curls into a sober pixie haircut, more suited, she thought, to travelling in the company of men. She shortened her nails, took a man's shirt from Andres's wardrobe, put it on the chair in the bedroom with a pair of black trousers and some moccasins, packed a few spare items, then went to bed.

In the morning, she dressed, made herself a sandwich, collected her bag and left without giving the house another glance. She walked to the dock, making sure to avoid the market where people knew her. When she reached the office, the dockers who had been working near the office the day before had left, leaving the place deserted. She knocked.

"Come in," the accented voice of the man rang in the silence.

She pushed open the tempered glass door, stepped into the room which seemed darker than she remembered from the day before, and called out a cautious hello. She couldn't distinguish anything at first. As her eyes began to get accustomed to the obscurity, she guessed the shape of the man sat in his chair behind the large wooden desk. The air was filled with a smell she hadn't noticed the previous day, a strong and familiar smell that filled her with unease. She could feel a throbbing pain growing below her left shoulder blade, where tension always gathered when Andres was due home from one of his trips. The ache distracted her for a second from the dim surrounding, long enough that the blinding brightness of the desk lamp coming on startled her. She blinked a few times, willing her eyes to focus on the glistening face of the man from the day before. A faint movement in the shadow made her eye draw an arc to something behind the faux-leather office chair. That smell again, stronger. Chaotic thoughts collided in her mind as she tried to locate that scent. There. Andres's *Brillantine* hair wax. Her whole body vibrated with fear, as her husband emerged from the shadows.

Andres tilted his head over his left shoulder, turning towards the docker.

"Thanks for the call Tío," he said, "*Mi mujer* gets confused. I'll take her home now."

He drew a right hand and clasped the man's assured fingers into a hard handshake. With his other hand, he ripped the wedge of money Marianne had been holding close to her chest and pocketed it, handing his share to Tío. Before Marianne could react, he grabbed the gun wrapped in cloth. "I'll take that back, *mujer*. You don't want to hurt yourself."

Stepping forward, he pulled Marianne's shortened hair and yanked her through the door. Outside, Marianne saw the pale blue T-Bird, she had failed to notice before, parked between two stacks of containers.

At the house, Andres dragged Marianne up the stairs, threw her on the floor, slapping her to keep still. She saw him reach for his gun and a numbness came over her body. This is it, she thought. He grabbed the weapon by the barrel and brought the grip down on her face, over and over, kicking her body as he did. She tried to block his blows at first, but it only made him redouble his efforts. In the end, she just lay there, staring at the carpet. She lost track of time, minutes replaced by the rhythmic pounding that tore at her insides, again, and again, and again.

When he finally grew tired, he raised her bloodied head towards him, and between gritted teeth threatened, "Look what you made me do, *mujer*. Embarrass me like that again and I will kill you."

Cardiff

My treatment ended at the hospital, and I moved into a shared rented house off City Road. My housemate was a locum optometrist, a girl with a singing Yorkshire accent who spent half of the week on the road, and the rest at her boyfriend's flat. Her ephemeral presence suited me. I had retrained as a translator and now mostly worked from home. A corner of the lounge served as a small office, with a desk facing the window to the back garden. I worked mornings, seven days a week. In the afternoon, I took an hour's walk, a routine the hospital doctor had recommended, arguing the virtues of both nature and exercise to keep a healthy mind. I chose a different route each day, but always ended my circuit in the same little coffee shop.

Several times a week I exchanged messages with Leandro. By email at first, with the occasional call on Skype. For several months now he'd been looking into my mother's past in Colombia, doing research in between his other projects, using his many contacts as an investigative journalist to retrace her steps. He would call me when he had found something and I would keep a record in my notebook, slowly pulling threads together. He rang just to say hi other times, our exchanges part of an increasingly familiar routine that grounded me. His face, the sound of his voice. Even though he was thousands of miles away, or maybe because of the distance, his presence gave me a renewed appetite for human connections.

As I reached the café that day, the enthusiastic barista dressed in a Welsh rugby top welcomed me with a smile and a heavily accented *bonjour*.

"*Shwmae*," I replied. "*Un paned o de, os gwelwch yn dda.*"

"Ah, *da iawn*. Very good. We'll make a Welsh speaker out of you yet," she commented, nodding approvingly. "Sit, sit. I'll bring it to you now. We've got one of your fellow countrymen here today. Maybe you know each other?" She pointed at a man with floppy hair sat at the back.

"I doubt that. Been gone a long time, you know," I cringed

internally, scanning the busy café for a free table. Only one was free, wedged between a young couple stealing glances at their phones whilst talking, and the floppy-haired man, absorbed in what looked like a crime novel based on the cover design. Definitely French, I thought. Sighing, I squeezed between them and reached the empty seat. I unpacked the content of my rucksack onto the wooden surface, sat on the padded burgundy chair, and started to transcribe notes from my most recent conversation with Leandro, headphones playing Benjamin Barber's *Agnus Dei*.

"Are you writing a book?"

Startled, I moved one headphone off my right ear. Cable dangling, I made eye contact with the man to my right. "Sorry?"

He placed his novel face down on the wooden table. The spine showed little sign of wear, I noticed.

"Are you writing a book?" He was looking right at me, his finger pointing at the screen.

"Not quite, more like a journal," I replied, wondering how much detail would seem normal.

"What's it about?" he asked. I detected the amplified intonations of a *banlieusard*, behind his comedic French accent.

"Travel," I replied, hoping that my English was good enough to hide our common nationality. I wasn't quite ready for the sort of contrived expat-abroad conversations in which distance erased all social conventions.

"Are you an, *une adventurière*?"

I cringed. "You mean an explorer? No, not quite. More an observer." – This wasn't going very well – "More like threads of memories." – Christ, too detailed.

The man looked at me blankly.

"Family. I'm writing about family travel." I wondered what it was about this man that made me want to justify myself. In the past I would have simply blanked him. I noticed that his eyes were scanning the text on the screen. Flustered by the intrusion, I slammed my laptop shut and reached for the notebook in my bag.

"Look, I don't mean to be rude, but I came here to work. Do you mind? Sorry."

Argh! Why did I feel the need to apologise? Such a British quirk. Anyway, the man seemed to take the hint and retreated into his book, emitting an incoherent grumble. I made an exaggerated show of putting my headphones back on and gulped a mouthful of milky tea. Cold. Shit. Frowning, I opened the notebook and tracked my small handwriting, looking for a line, trying to recall what Leandro had said that had seemed significant. No. It was gone. The effort it had taken to hold this brief exchange had drained me. There was nothing left but to pack and head home.

Outside, a fine drizzle swallowed me into its muggy mist. Great, I thought, rummaging in my rucksack for the little foldable umbrella I always kept in there. "Bugger," I exclaimed, cheeks warm with irritation. "Bus it is." I jogged to the bus stop, covering the bag containing my laptop inside my coat like a new-born. From a distance, I spotted a tall moustachioed man under the bus shelter. Something about his appearance made me slow down. The way he stood, maybe. People caught in the rain instinctively slouched to fend off the elements. This man carried himself straight, too straight; seemingly unaware of the damp patches spreading across his shoulders, to his upper arms, revealing the hint of a tattoo. Wearily, I stepped next to him, avoiding his gaze, scanning the road, searching for a sign of the bus in the distance. I spotted it, eagerly stepping onto the road. The rain had redoubled by now, gluing hair to the back of my neck.

"*Vous allez loin?*" the man asked, startling me. When I looked, he had moved beside me and stood uncomfortably close "*Le bus.* Do you have far to travel?"

I shrugged, acting as if I couldn't understand. I didn't have another conversation in me. As the bus pulled over, the thudding of blood pumping in my ears covered the sound of the engine. I took another step forward into the rain, no longer caring about the laptop. I waved at the conductor and the concertina doors slammed open. I climbed on, purchased a ticket and manoeuvred towards the back of the bus. It was empty this time of day. Only once the door had slammed shut and the bus pulled away did I look back. The man stood where I had left him, eyes firmly locked onto mine. Creep, I thought.

By the time I reached home, the rain had stopped. My hair was dripping, my clothes creased from sitting in the steamed-up bus. I emptied the contents of the damp bag onto the desk, plugged the laptop in, hung the bag to dry in the kitchen, peeled off my wet clothes and threw them in the washing machine. Briefly, I considered the machine's many dials, deciding on a bath first.

A loud ringing jerked me out of sleep. I must have dozed off. A little groggy from my nap, my hand mechanically reached for the familiar shape of the mobile phone on the bedside table. Finding it, I lifted the brightly lit home screen to my face. The time showed: 12.34 am am. It took a few more seconds for me to realise the sound was coming from the landline. Nobody ever rang that number. I thought about my mother, trying to repress the sense of dread. Trying to anchor myself, I stood up, wrapped a towel around myself and wobbled to the bedroom on spaghetti legs. On the mantlepiece stood the receiver. I picked it up and pressed the answer button.

"Hello?"

The line was dead. I typed the call back number that was written on the back of the phone.

"Number withheld," came the automated voice.

I looked at the clock again. 12.37 am. Who could be ringing at this hour? I tried Leandro's number, unsure what time it would be in Rio by now. The call went to voicemail.

"Probably working," I said, out loud, finding the sound of my own voice reassuring somehow. "Not going back to sleep now." I wrapped myself in a white dressing gown resting on the bedframe.

Catching a glimpse of my dark circled eyes in the mirror, I headed downstairs.

When my housemate was absent, I never put the heating on at night. The kitchen felt like a walk-in freezer. Tea, I thought. I filled the electric kettle, placed it on its stand, and flicked the switch. Whilst the water warmed, I grabbed a clean cup from the cupboard and added a sachet of camomile tea. Good for the nerves, I thought. When I heard the water bubbling up, I switched off the kettle and poured as much water as the cup would contain. Picking up the drink, I hugged the porcelain with both hands, waiting for the heat to diffuse its soothing warmth through my fingers. Might as well work, I sighed.

The lounge was in complete darkness. From the door, I couldn't see the little flashing LED of the dormant laptop, which usually illuminated the room with an eerie blue glow. Still holding onto the cup with both hands to prevent a spill, I pushed with my elbow towards the light switch. I strained at my shoulder to reach the necessary height, brushing the wall in a sweeping movement. Instead of the hard, cold surface of the switch, my elbow connected with something soft, warm. A human warmth. Terrified, I jumped back, pushing both arms in front of me in defence, hurtling my drink towards the invisible intruder. I heard the shattering sound the cup made as it hit the floor then something hard struck the back of my head, plunging me into darkness.

I opened my eyes to find a ray of sunshine drawing an elongated line on the parquet flooring. My face felt warm and sticky. The short hand on my watch pointed to six o'clock. A metallic taste made me pat my whole body for signs of injury. The persistent throbbing on the back of my head brought a flash of recollection, the feeling of a heavy object coming down on my skull. I sat up urgently from the cold floor. Was the intruder still in the house? Scanning the room for clues, I registered the empty desk. The laptop and my notebook were gone. I stood up, looking around for other signs of burglary, moving cautiously up the stairs, checking the windows, the cupboard, my housemate's room, circling back to the front door, which was locked. The intruder, whoever he was, had long gone, I finally concluded.

Upstairs, I collapsed on the bed. After a few minutes, I raised myself up to examine the bedraggled reflection in front of the full-length mirror. My hair was sticking up in all directions, a clump of it caked in blood over my left temple, rivulets of coagulated red stuff coating my left ear, trickling down my neck and onto my now crimson-streaked dressing gown. With one hand, I patted the hard bulge of my skull, finding a gash. A cursory review of the substance on my fingers told me the blood had long dried. Still, I called 999.

Half an hour later, a police car pulled up outside. Two officers entered the house, commenting on the absence of signs of effraction. Eyebrows knitted together, they recorded my statement. "Your accent. Where is it from?" the older one asked.

"France," I told him. "But I have lived in Wales most of my adult life."

"I love Paris," the younger female officer said, visibly mellowing. "I'm desperate for my partner to take us there."

I had expected someone to take prints, like in the movies. Instead, I was given a leaflet for Victims Support. After that, they simply left. It was unlikely anyone would be caught, they warned me. The old officer had directed his questioning in a manner that made me wonder if he thought, maybe, this was an insurance scam. No signs of break-in, he kept saying. Was it not strange all that was missing was the laptop and a notebook, when the plasma TV that belonged to my housemate had been left intact? The woman had been more sympathetic, pointing at my bloodied head and offering to request an ambulance. Someone ought to check that nasty gash. I'd thanked her, but no.

After their departure, I recalled the two French men who had accosted me the previous day. Had I been under some sort of surveillance? And if so, why? As if on autopilot, I got up, washed the blood off my hair with a cloth, bandaged it up and dressed in a pair of baggy jeans and a grey hoodie.

Outside, the rain was back. I pulled the hood of my coat up and walked to Central Station. It was rush hour. The platform busy.

"Single to Paddington, please." I told the conductor, handing him my credit card.

In London, I took the underground to New Cavendish Street where I stood in front of the familiar wooden door, painted black, decorated with a golden handle in the shape of a lion's head. Turning towards the intercom, I pressed the top buzzer.

"Who is it?" enquired a voice in an American accent.

"Charlotte. Can I come in?"

As I ascended the stairs to the top floor apartment, I hesitated. Max and I had seldom spoken since he'd sent the box. Recently, I'd been absorbed in my enquiries with Leandro. I felt guilty now. Max had been steadfast, a familiar mooring, but he was my father's best friend, and thus a painful reminder.

Rabat

After Francis's funeral, Marianne felt the need to return to Rabat. First, she visited the tomb of her father. He had died young, before Morocco's independence. A man who embodied a different era. Driven by the new opportunities that colonies offered an entrepreneurial man with otherwise limited prospects in the metropole. What had it all been for in the end? He had died alone, estranged from his wife and children.

Marianne took a taxi, searching for Avenue du Maréchal Joffre, the street on which her childhood home had stood. The taxi driver was a wrinkled old man who spoke an elegant French. He remembered the name, explained that after the independence, all the names had been changed. As he parked, he offered to wait for Marianne, concern painted on his leathered face for this unaccompanied elderly woman who seemed so out of place. She thanked him, said she knew the area well, and urged him on.

A new building stood where the white house had once been. There, her mother's Royal poodles had slept on the terrace at night. There, Jean had convinced her it would be funny to throw sun-dried dog poo at unsuspecting passers-by as children. She smiled, remembering her mother's fury when a neighbour had ratted them out. Her crimson face as she hobbled on one foot after the two truants, taking aim with her *babouche*, failing to catch them as they disappeared in the back garden. The death of Francis was raising many ghosts, so many that Marianne started to question whether she had not died herself. Turning the street corner, she was frightened by the ethereal shape of two Moroccan women in black veils brushing past her as if she were invisible.

In one of the city museums, she found a plaque which read: *The land that covers the Kingdom of Morocco has been inhabited since the Lower Palaeolithic. From 1912 to 1956, Morocco was a French Protectorate. Under French rule, bones dated 300,000 years old were excavated in Jebel Irhoud. At the time, they constituted the oldest example of Homo Sapiens discovered anywhere in the world.* Only forty-four years, yet this had been the place of her birth, and her home, once.

No longer, she realised. Morocco had become a foreign country.

Meknes

During her parents' divorce Marianne was sent to live in Meknes with family friends. There, she had developed a friendship with the daughter, Louise, a friendship built on a shared love of walking, and painting, that would see them scouring Parisian museums together late into their eighties. The two girls were inseparable. Every day, they would walk home from school, stopping to buy *cornes de gazelle* – little almond cakes flavoured with orange blossom water and wrapped in sugar. On sunny days, they headed to the public pool to watch boys from another school outdo themselves on the diving board, whilst they paraded in their colourful bathing suits, two fifteen-year-olds eager for attention.

Leaving the pool one day, the two friends were cackling about a boy who had just asked Louise to the dance the following Saturday. Ahead of them, a clamour rose, echoed by swelling cries from all over the city. Turning the corner towards Louise's house, they were met by a line of Moroccan men, fists raised, shouting a slogan in Arabic. Amongst them was a boy not much older than they were, waving a red and green flag. A forbidden flag. Muted, the girls exchanged a look and Louise grabbed Marianne by the sleeve, pulling her into a doorway. The two girls huddled against each other, watching as dozens of angry men marched past, ignoring them, a hive carried by an instinctual motivation. The girls spoke enough of the language to understand what they were calling for: the departure of the French occupiers. Hearing those words, they made themselves smaller, wishing not to be seen. Long after the last man had passed, they tentatively regained the pavement, eyes sweeping left and right. Silent.

Louise's mother was waiting at the door. She ushered them into the courtyard, threw a cautious look into the road, and, finding it empty, locked the heavy door behind them. Louise described their experience as an uprising. Her father dismissed it as an isolated

164

incident. A week later, Marianne was called back to Rabat where life resumed as before. Her mother remarried to a surgeon, and over time it was as if her father had never existed.

Cartagena

Marianne had appeared to Francis, dressed in a pair of white trousers, wide at the leg, and a similarly coloured linen blouse held tight around the waist with a wide buckled brown leather belt. Her arms were adorned with wide golden bracelets that exuded the confidence of a more mature woman than the girl he remembered. Still, and despite the large sunglasses, he recognised her straight away.

He had been waiting for her in front of a small antiquarian, a distance away from her house. Moving past him, she entered the shop. He hung back a moment longer, eyeing the handful of passers-by. Inside, he had nodded in the direction of a wrinkled old shopkeeper. She was dressed in colourful beads which contrasted with her severe bun of grey hair. The elderly lady had manoeuvred away from her till, lifting a wooden flap between two glass cabinets showcasing jewellery labelled Mexican silver, and moved towards Marianne, in a flurry of brightly dyed skirts that reminded her of a flamenco dancer.

"More silver jewellery upstairs, señora," she had announced, taking Marianne by the arm, and directing her towards the steps. They headed for a small staircase at the back, leading to an area marked 'staff only'.

Marianne had glanced at the woman, uncertain. The woman had nodded, encouragingly. "Sí, sí, señora."

Francis spoke a few words, addressed to Marianne in French. Her eyes narrowed. "*No te reconozco,*" she replied, cautious. I don't know who you are. "This is a mistake." As she said it, she turned and motioned to leave.

"Marianne," he called.

She paused, hesitant, turned, and moved closer, scrutinising the man's face like the Holy Inquisitor. "Francis? *C'est vraiment toi?*" she asked, in the uncertain French of a woman no longer used to her own maternal tongue. He nodded. She reached for his face, patting it as if to dispel an apparition. "How?"

They sat in silence, surrounded by dusty trinkets, each sizing the other one up. It had been years. People changed.

"I heard you went to London," Francis finally said, breaking the silence. "How did you end up here, in Colombia?"

Marianne told him about her training, the job with Avianca. She spoke in one breath, without pause.

"Then I met Andres ... I was still a child. I didn't see ..." Andres's name had triggered an instinctive response. She looked at her watch, stood up. "I have to go now."

Francis reached up, taking hold of her folded forearm. "Meet me again. Here next week."

She looked down at his hand as if at an unlikely ghost.

"We can't ..." she said, almost as if he were a child, a naive child. "You don't know ..." Her voice trailed off.

"I know ..."

For the first time in his life, he broke protocol. He told her about his work for the SDECE, about various posts he had held in North Africa. She was easy to talk to, like a familiar memory. "And now I'm here," he added.

"Why South America?" she asked, sounding sceptical. "I mean, do you even speak Spanish?"

Francis chuckled. "You know, I wondered the same thing until I saw you ... I suspect your cousin Elizabeth had a hand in my transfer."

On hearing Elizabeth's name, Marianne's eyebrows rose. "I see," she said. "And the operation you talk about ... it has something to do with Andres's other ... activities?"

He nodded. Soon after, she said she needed to leave.

"Promise to meet again. In a week. Give me a week."

Marianne agreed.

When he felt it was safe to do so, Francis arranged another meeting with Marianne at the little shop.

"And your business with my husband?" she asked.

He registered the disdain in her voice. "It is complicated. What matters is that I can help."

"You say that. What makes you think I need help?"

There she was. The old Marianne he knew. Defiant. He pointed at the bruises around her wrist. She covered the marks with her hand.

"I can get you out of Colombia."

"I have tried." As she said it, Francis noticed the tightening of her jaw.

"I can get you fake papers, a flight for France."

She said nothing to that.

"I will find a way," he insisted. He could see the hint of dark circles under the skilfully applied make-up. He held her hand and squeezed gently. "Trust me Marianne."

"Let me think about it," she replied, pulling from under his grip and getting up.

At their next meeting, Francis told Marianne of his plan. "We shouldn't meet again. Be ready. I'll have a silver necklace delivered to your house. It will be your signal."

The next drug shipment was to be their window. Once it arrived, Andres would travel to Venezuela to accompany the new merchandise all the way to Miami, giving Francis a few days to extract Marianne from Colombia. That's what he called it, an extraction. CIA agents would be waiting to pick up Andres at Miami airport, he told her.

"We will be travelling as husband and wife," he added. "It will help us blend in."

Unconvinced, Marianne explained about the dock master's betrayal. Francis took the revelation with a frown.

"I wondered how Tío had managed to gain Andres's trust," he let out.

Marianne shivered at the comment.

"As long as we use the airspace between Colombia and Miami,

we won't be able to blend in," she warned again. "Andres has contacts everywhere. He pays well. We will be betrayed."

"On a commercial flight, sure." Francis replied, an enigmatic smile on his lips. "Have faith."

Marianne heard the rumbling sound of a car parking on the opposite side of the street from the house in Cartagena, engine kept running. She waited, tuning in to listen for any unfamiliar sound. When she heard none, she made her way to the front door. She unlocked the deadbolt quietly with one hand, stepped outside, and crossed the front garden to the metal gate guarding the entrance to the villa. There, she paused, holding her breath, listening for the sounds of the night. A stream fluttering nearby, the gentle rustling of leaves in the tree, a dog, barking in the distance. No human sound, just the ragged rhythm of her own breath, and the car engine, within reach. Marianne pushed the iron gate open, holding it up to prevent the rusty hinges from emitting their strident shriek. In the street, she paused once more, scanning the shadows for any sign of movement, smelling the air. She covered the few steps to the waiting car, opened the passenger door, and slid next to the driver.

"You came," she told Francis.

They drove in silence from Route 90 to Maicao and the Venezuelan border. Marianne stared out the window at the unfurling landscape, thinking about the little blue note she had found in her pocket a few weeks earlier. An address in Cartagena, scribbled in pencil. A time. And on the back one word: Chouara.

Marianne had blinked repeatedly at the reference to the tannery, wondering if this was a joke from Andres to torment her. But no, she had never mentioned anything about that summer to him. To anyone.

Before they reached the control post, Francis checked his rear-view mirror for any signs they might have been followed, then parked the car on a side lane. Reaching for something behind Marianne's seat, he retrieved a black leather travelling bag, unzipped it and pulled out two passports. The first, he pocketed, handing her the other. "If a patrolman asks any questions, we are a French couple on holiday travelling around central America."

From the bag he pulled out a bundle of other documents. "Travel insurance and *livret de famille*. It adds to the credibility. Do you have any questions?" he asked, with the attention of a pedagogue.

She shook her head.

Francis turned the key into the ignition and restarted the engine, manoeuvring a U-turn to rejoin the *autopista 90*.

Eventually, bright lights appeared in the distance. She saw a man in customs uniform waving at them to reduce speed. Francis slowed the car to a halt, and calmly cranked down his window, taking his passport from his shirt pocket. Marianne mimicked him, pulling hers from her handbag.

"Good evening, officer," he announced, chirpily, handing the documents through the open window to the uniformed man.

"What is your business in Venezuela, Señor?" the uniformed man asked, sternly.

"I promised my wife to take her to visit Maracaibo."

Marianne looked at Francis. Who was that man who bent the truth with such ease? Was she making a mistake following him?

The officer grunted; eyes fixed on the passport photographs. He bent his knees and moved his head backwards, to gain a better perspective of the passenger seat. Marianne held her breath and smiled. She thought she perceived hesitation in his look.

"*Bueno*," he said finally, closing the passports and handing them back to Francis.

He motioned them to move forward. Francis closed the window, handed the passports to Marianne, and started the car. Once they were moving, she let go of a deep sigh.

"It isn't over yet," he told her.

"This is further than I've been in years," she replied, heart pounding in her chest.

Francis drove the 600 kilometers to a port near Maracaibo, only stopping a few times to buy food. As they approached, Marianne's body stiffened, remembering the docks in Cartagena. When the car stopped near Maracaibo, Marianne felt her insides contract. "I don't know if I can do this," she whispered.

"Trust me," Francis replied. Stepping out of the car, he moved towards the passenger door and held it open, offering Marianne his hand. "This way."

Bogotà

At the same time, in Bogotà, there was a knock on the door.

"Come in," Max called with his booming voice.

The young military aide walked in, tucking a clipboard under his armpit to salute.

"At ease, son." Max said.

"Sir, the plane has just been apprehended. We have the men in custody. Nineteen in total," he read from the clipboard.

"Excellent," Max replied. "Any news from the team?"

"Not yet, sir."

"Right, let me know when you do."

"Certainly, sir."

Max sat back into his chair, rubbing his neck.

The phone rang and he picked up mechanically.

"Sir? We have a problem," the voice of the aide sounded stiff.

"Do tell."

"Our men have vanished, sir."

Max felt his neck tense. "What do you mean vanished?"

"Francis is reported to have rented a car a few hours ago, and nobody has seen him since."

"Right. And what about Tío?"

"He was due to go back to his office in the docks so as not to arouse suspicion. Nobody has seen him, sir."

"I see."

"Sir, another thing," the aide hesitated. "It is a little strange actually."

"What?" Max barked down the phone. He hated being drip-fed information.

"Andres's wife is also missing, sir."

Max got up, massaging his sore neck. He hated being blindsided. He started to pace the room in concentric circles, called the aide.

"Stick to protocol. Bring me all the surveillance notes we have on Andres and Tío. The wife too."

The aide returned a few minutes later with a pile of colourful folders, all stamped with the CIA logo and the words CONFIDENTIAL in red lettering.

"Leave them there," Max pointed at a corner of his desk. "I don't want to be disturbed."

He walked back to his desk, sat in front of the pile of documents and sieved through the surveillance notes his team had gathered, pulling out anything which mentioned Andres's wife.

It was late in the night when Max emerged from his office, a stack of loose papers clutched in his right hand.

"Put those in an envelope for me and find me Francis and Tío's full military files," he ordered.

"Yes, sir." The young lad was glad to stretch his legs. He reappeared a few minutes later. "Here, sir." He placed two green folders and a brown envelope on the desk.

Max leafed at pace through the files, looking for something specific. "There!" he shouted. "There," he repeated, regaining his usual composure. He placed the files side by side, pulling out a third one from the surveillance folder. "Do you believe in coincidences, son?" he called to his aide through the door.

"No, sir."

Nor did Max. Yet in all three files was a recurring word: Rabat. That couldn't be good.

Max's phone rang again. "Now what?"

"Sir, we just received word. Andres has managed to escape, sir."

Replacing the receiver, he stood up, grabbed the envelope and put on his jacket.

"Go home, son. There is something I need to do."

7. MOSAIC

Rio de Janeiro

The distant double chime of a Skype call resonates from the bedside table, bringing the phone to life. Half asleep, Leandro stretches his arm to grab his mobile, accepting the call with one swift swipe of the thumb. "Charlotte? Is everything alright?" he asks the now familiar contour of her face on the framed screen. "I missed your call?" He is speaking in the generalised international language that acts as a bridge between his Portuguese and her French, an imperfect tool that has nonetheless served them well these past few months. He often wonders if their relationship would have been different if either of them had spoken the other's language. As it stands, they can only offer each other an interpreted version of themselves, mediated through English. What he first considered a linguistic impairment has had the benefit of shearing the superfluous. He likes that their exchanges are simple and true; condensed to their very essence.

From her initial email, Leandro had imagined Charlotte like a grey library bat with hair mounted in a chignon, not the slender brunette that materialised on his screen the first time they video called. He would have liked to chat with her a little longer, even then, but she was focused, eager for answers, armed with a name and the pixelated picture of an old man in a blue shirt, printed from a magazine in a language she did not even speak. Yes, he was the author of the article. And yes, Andres was incarcerated in Venezuela still. She had more questions. About another arrest. Another time. And about an escape. How had Andres escaped? Who had helped him? Where had he been all this time?

Over time, Leandro grew intrigued by this intense woman, attuned to the way her upper lip quivered each time he replied to her that he didn't know. She kept pushing. There might have been another man. Max had definitely mentioned another agent. Yes, he'd finally said, dredging his memory for details. A man with a peculiar nickname, he had added. Father or something. No, Uncle. That was it, *Uncle*. Her upper lip had trembled. Not the name she was expecting. Then something had passed across her face. *Ingles o español?* What was she asking? Was his name in English, she'd clarified? No. Tío. His nickname was Tío. Her face had become animated then, blood pooling in her cheeks. She'd leant forward, moving closer to the screen, closer to Leandro. What did he know about Tío? Very little, *deux têtes*. It was how you said it in French, wasn't it? Top of my head? No, she'd replied, *de tête* – short 'e' sound. Otherwise, you mean *two heads*. Like two heads together? That works too, Leandro had grinned until he'd realised Charlotte didn't look amused, flicking the air with the back of her hand, as you would swat a fly. Sorry, he'd said, promising to look in his archives. He had wanted to ask more questions. He'd be back in touch, very soon. Her lips had drawn the beginning of a smile.

Andres, the man Charlotte had initially written about in her email, was a criminal, a man possessed by greed whose murky career had culminated in an extravagant escape. He had spent a life making himself invisible, running small drug trades from a village in Venezuela. The other man, Tío, was more elusive. Leandro had come across the odd reference whilst researching his book, but nobody knew the man's real name, or where he had come from. Leandro's file had contained very little. He could have emailed Charlotte to say as much, but she was already a puzzle, one he was eager to solve.

"You said your mother was Andres's wife?" he asked when they next arranged a video call. "That must have been long ago?"

"Sixty years, give or take," she'd replied.

"And you ... you want to meet the man or what?"

"It's complicated."

"Try me."

"She ... told me he was dead."

"Your mother? Maybe she had her reasons? The man is no saint, you know. Those guys, they're dangerous. Maybe you'd better let it lie?"

"A strange thing for a journalist to say."

He had smiled. "I suppose. You seem like a nice person, that's all."

Her eyes had lingered off screen. "I need to know ... There are too many gaps already."

He'd watched her face narrow. He could see the pain in those grey-blue eyes.

"Won't you help me?"

Leandro had noticed the way Charlotte's face had imperceptibly hardened, like someone anticipating a blow. There definitely was something about her, the way she held her head high, her jaw clamped. Defiant. At the same time, haunted, vulnerable. He reminded himself she had tracked him down from halfway around the world, and without speaking much Portuguese. He had started enquiries with a lot less. "Why don't you start at the beginning?" he had finally said.

Over the course of a dozen calls, Charlotte told Leandro everything she had uncovered, everything Max had told her too. Max, the family friend who turned out to be a CIA operative. That had pricked his attention. He had long suspected the Latin Connection to have links to the French Intelligence Community. That would explain why they always seemed to be one step ahead. Looking into Charlotte's mother, it had been easy enough to find her employment records and marriage certificate, but after that the trail had gone cold. He had left messages with reporter friends he knew in Colombia and Venezuela, but it took time for people to get back to him. Other stories came along, and he was often away, travelling to report for his magazine.

Wherever he was, he would try to keep in touch with Charlotte, keeping her abreast of his lack of progress to date. Once they started to use WhatsApp video calls, his eyes would lock on her upper lip, anticipating the fluttering that increasingly made his chest tighten.

179

"This is hopeless," she concluded after months of no further leads.

He noticed her eyes were glistening.

"I've been wasting your time. I'm sorry, Leandro."

It was the first time she had seemed defeated. His heartbeat quickened.

"Maybe we should just stop?" Her tone was deflated.

"No," he pleaded, before she could take another breath.

Her eyes sharpened then, as if she was the one reading him now.

"I mean," he hesitated. "I mean, there are other avenues we can explore."

"Like what? None of your colleagues have heard of Tío, and Andres is in jail. There's literally no one else we can ask."

"You could try your mother?" he hazarded.

"No. No, no," she replied, shaking her head vigorously.

"Ok," he raised his palms at the screen in defence. "Just a suggestion."

"I've thought about what you said. You're right, my mother must have had her reasons for lying. It's best she doesn't know what we're up to. And maybe it's best he doesn't find out about her either."

There was a pause, then Leandro took a deep inhale. "Maybe we've been looking at this all wrong."

"What do you mean?"

"Well, we know your parents were both involved, and we know Max told you everything he knows already."

"More or less."

"Yes, as much as you're going to get from a spook," he chuckled.

"Obviously." She rolled her eyes.

"So, it leaves Tío himself, who we obviously can't find ..."

"Yes?"

"...and Andres."

"Who is locked up in a Venezuelan prison."

"Exactly!"

"You've lost me."

"We know exactly where to find him ... I can go and visit Andres."

"But you can't. We just said ... I don't want to put my mother in danger."

"You, visiting him, might put her in danger. But I'm just a Brazilian journalist following up on a story about the Cosa Nostra in Latin America."

"You'd do that?"

"We want answers, don't we?"

"*We* do," she replied. "Oh, thank you, Leandro."

"Don't thank me yet. He might not agree to meet, and it is going to require *a lot* of paperwork."

"I know," Charlotte said. "I'm thanking you for giving it a go."

"We're together in this now."

For months Leandro followed a lengthy administrative trail. From his office in Rio, he sought the necessary permissions, liaising with the Venezuelan consulate. His journalist's credentials opened some doors, two envelopes filled with cash did the rest. He reported to Charlotte daily now, through a stream of messages posted to her email inbox, like footsteps between two time zones.

The night before the prison visit, Leandro stayed in a motel the prison office had directed him to. Lying on the bed, he was rehearsing a line of questioning in his head when the phone rang.

"Charlotte, is everything ok? I missed your call."

"Did I wake you? I wanted to hear your voice."

"I'm here. Look," he waved his hand at the screen, "you can see me."

"I wish I had come with you."

"It's not safe, Charlotte. Especially after the break-in and the theft of your laptop. We've obviously rattled someone."

"I know. You just feel so far away."

"No more than before. Besides, it is only for another week."

"How so?"

He cleared his throat. "There is a conference in London on Drug Cartels in a Global Economy. My paper approved the travel plans yesterday. I'll be in the UK in a few days."

"In London? Really? You mean ..."

"I mean that we can meet there, in person." For a moment, the picture seemed to freeze. "Charlotte? Are you there?"

"Here, really?" Her voice had shrunk to a whisper.

Leandro nodded, a wide grin on his face.

"Sure. Is that ok? Me coming to London, I mean?"

"I think so. I mean yes. Yes, of course. I never ... you know?"

"Thought we would be in the same time zone?" He laughed.

"Right?" She mirrored his smile. "I mean, it is going to be weird," she gesticulated, grabbing clumps of her hair. "There are so many places I want to show you."

"There'll be time," he promised. "I'd better say goodnight now. Long day tomorrow."

"Incredible," she replied, almost to herself. Then quieter, "Leandro?"

"Yes, Charlotte?"

"I am really glad I met you. You're the best."

"Me too, Charlotte. I feel the universe planned for us to meet."

Charlotte felt a flutter in her chest. "Can we stay on the line a little longer?" she said, in a tentative voice.

"I'd like that," he replied, softly. He placed down the mobile on the pillow next to his head and closed his eyes.

"Good night, Leandro."

"Good night, Charlotte."

Through the phone speaker, Charlotte listened to the soft purring of Leandro's respiration, the sound like a warm blanket wrapped across her shoulders. It was already daytime in Cardiff. Leandro was the closest thing Charlotte had to a friend, she realised. The way he'd offered to help. Nobody had displayed this sort of kindness towards her for a very long time. Only Max, but he was her father's best friend. Leandro was different. Young. Handsome. Of course, she'd noticed his symmetrical features and the intensity of his gaze. She liked the way he seemed to drink her face in, at a safe distance still. Five thousand miles away. Far enough that even *she* couldn't mess things up.

Cardiff

What had made me contact Leandro in Brazil? A thirst to understand a past that kept fizzling away. Maybe. Or the need to invent a connection, however elusive, with my mother, or the part of her I knew nothing about. It was as if we belonged to neighbouring countries. That space between us, it made me feel hollow, like a piece was missing. Andres was the key. After receiving the box from Max, I had convinced myself that if I learnt about him, about Andres and my mother's life with him, a likeness would materialise, a picture in which I would recognise myself.

Leandro had seemed guarded at first. After all, I could be anyone. A crazy person raving about a character in an article he had written.

I had imagined that in the course of his research, he would have come across more details about my mother, details that had seemed irrelevant for his book, but might be meaningful to me.

"I'm sorry," he'd replied. "I didn't even know the man had been married." I must have looked disappointed for he added, "You do know what sort of character Andres is, don't you?"

Months of Skype and email exchanges with Leandro had changed something, however. Changed me. Something about his loyalty. Despite the physical distance between us, or maybe thanks to it.

"Why did you become an investigative journalist," I asked him one day.

"I make it my mission to expose the association between organised crime and local politicians," he replied as if reciting an elevator pitch.

"That's your stock answer. I've got loads of those," I scolded. "I'm asking what's your story, Leandro. What makes you risk your life to expose those people?"

That's when he told me about Clara.

"She was a sweet girl I had watched growing up across the road from my parents'. My mother babysat her when she was a kid. Her parents were away often. She got besotted with this thug, a kid from the *barrio* who ran with older boys. They all thought they were big men, important because they did the odd job for the cartel. Delivery boys mostly. I knew most of them by sight. We all did. And then one day, Clara was with her boyfriend when his crew turned up. They had a job. His initiation, they called it. The older boy, the one in charge, said it wouldn't take long. The rest is like a bad cliché. Clara tried to leave. The older boy insisted he'd walk her, for protection, he said. The boyfriend just ... let them go." On screen, Leandro's image seemed to freeze.

"Are you still here?" I asked. I saw a movement. A shudder. He raised his hand, as if to be counted.

"Her body. Her body was found three days later in a shallow grave outside our village. Her dress was soaked in her own blood. Her face unrecognisable. The boyfriend was never seen again."

"Did they arrest someone?"

"My mother accompanied our neighbour to the station. She told the policemen who had committed this atrocity. They did nothing. Said there was not enough evidence. Everyone knew."

"Oh Leandro, I'm so sorry."

"So, you see, someone has to speak out. To tell the truth."

"What happened after that?"

"I moved to São Paulo to study. Journalism school."

"And then?"

"Then I went back to the village, tracked down the boys, uncovered links between the traffickers and the local police chief. Blew the whole cartel open. It was my article which got the Latin Connection dismantled."

"The Latin Connection as in Andres's organisation?"

Leandro nodded.

"You mean you helped get him arrested?"

"I suppose I did, in a roundabout way."

"Then what?"

"There are many Claras in this life ... so I became an investigative reporter."

I couldn't help feeling impressed by a man who had dedicated his life to uncovering injustices, however unlikely a knight in shining armour he seemed in his black t-shirt and washed-out denim jacket. Another time, he told me about growing up mixed race in the favelas. He talked about the mothers' determination to raise men with good values who wouldn't get tangled with the gangs. "They are formidable women, Charlotte. All of them," he said, a tear rolling from the corner of his eye. "They make the tough calls, so we don't repeat the mistakes of our fathers." He added that his mother had worked two jobs to send him to university. To give him a chance in life.

The way Leandro spoke about his mother was disarming. I felt genuinely moved by his capacity for empathy towards those he helped, and by the obvious love he had for his mother. Despite the distance, I felt I could see him whole, pieced together from those fragments he shared. More so maybe than if we had met in person.

Around me, I started to notice more of life. On my daily walk, I spotted a robin on a bench, chirping; laughed at a dog walker tangled in his lead; smiled at the teenage couple wrapped in a languorous embrace. A palette of rich emotions spread at my fingertips, giving new vibrancy to an otherwise regimented routine. I awaited the daily Skype call with impatient anticipation, checking the time with growing urgency. When Leandro's attentive face came on, when I heard the warm tones of his baritone voice, a flutter filled my chest. Over time, the distance that had felt safe at first, weighed heavy. More than anything, I wanted Leandro to find me.

Leandro

After his interview, Leandro journeyed directly from Venezuela, without returning to Brazil. He boarded a bus to the capital, blind to the densely packed conurbation, indifferent to the changing landscape. He was distracted. Too busy speaking to his office on the phone, asking for a flight change to be arranged. The voice of the newspaper administrator was phasing in and out with the patchy phone coverage. He couldn't take down the flight number. "Could you repeat one more time?" he asked, swallowing his mounting frustration. Finally, he caught the full number, thanked the voice on the other end of the line and hung up.

On the plane, Leandro couldn't eat, or sleep. His mind was effervescent. He didn't notice the way his left leg kept twitching, the deep sighs of the middle-aged man in the seat next to him, the way the man cleared his throat two or three times, whilst eyeing the colourful spreadsheet on his laptop. Leandro was absorbed in thoughts, in the revelation he had extracted from Andres, in the connection he had derived from it.

"Will you just stop?" the man next to him burst, his tone exasperated.

"Sorry," Leandro replied, becoming aware of his own leg. The man settled back in his seat, righteous. Satisfied.

Looking out the oval window for the first time, Leandro noticed the vast expanse of ocean below the plane wings. It looked tranquil from above. He wondered how many species must live under the surface, invisible to the human eye. He tried to focus on a single point, to drill into the water with the power of his mind, but the plane was moving too fast, the point here one moment, gone the next. After a while, sea and sky became indistinguishable. A blur. How much of what our eyes saw was our mind betraying us, he mused.

Leandro conjured up an image of Charlotte. Her face. Her hair. The colour of her eyes. It had only been a day since they last spoke. He had no idea how tall or short she might be, he realised. Or what sort of shoes she would wear. His vision of her had been entirely framed by the constraints of a screen, and by the elements she chose to share with him. He pictured an iceberg. What did he know really? She presented herself like one of those large unattached blocks of ice that floated along the ocean, like their own landmass, pulled by invisible currents. He thought about the causality she attributed to certain events in her past. The meaning she derived from them all. In many ways, she seemed blinded to her own life's possibilities, invisible to the affection that had grown between them, stuck in a family narrative fraught with violence and grief. What would happen once he gave her the key to untangle the truth? What would it mean for them? It was just that the story didn't start where she thought. Once he broke the silence her family had worked so hard to protect, would he lose her?

Below, the quiet surface of the water was disturbed by a sudden gust of wind. Foam rolled atop mounting waves, hinting at marine life. Two gulls glided under the metal carcass. He would reach land soon.

Charlotte

Standing at the arrival gates with a cardboard sign marked LEANDRO in bright green letters, I suddenly feel exposed. I spot him first, taller than I had imagined from our Skype exchanges. He is wearing dark blue jeans, trainers, and a black long-sleeve shirt, creased from the long journey. In the flesh, his skin is leathered and sun-kissed, like that of a man used to the outdoors, his face framed by a thick mop of black curly hair. His only luggage is a compact suitcase dragging behind him like a lazy tortoise. Unsure about the protocol, I present my hand for him to shake, distracted by the opal of his eyes.

"Charlotte," I say, the tone of my voice ringing too formal.

He points at the board still in my hand and smiles. "I figured." As he says it, he picks me up off the floor.

"Lovely to finally ... meet you ... is that the right term?" I say, awkwardly. He shows no sign of releasing his grip. Hesitant, I drop the board and lace my arms around his neck. My nostrils fill with the familiar scent of sandalwood.

We stay like that for a while, as if our bodies were reluctant to let go, oblivious to the ballet of weary travellers, oversized suitcases, and joyous reunions that surround us. Deaf to the buzzing sounds of overlapping announcements.

"You're here," I murmur.

"I am," he replies, placing his hand on my face, tracing its contour with two fingers.

"Come," I say when he returns me to the ground. I feel giddy like a little girl. Taking hold of his hand, I guide him towards the taxi rank. "Do you have a hotel reservation?"

He shakes his head no and steps into the cab. I follow him and give the driver a set of instructions. Sat side by side on the black leather banquette, I search for his hand and clasp it into mine.

"Where are we going?" he asks.

"Max is away. I have the keys."

At Max's apartment, Leandro asks if he can take a shower.

"I'll fix us some sandwiches," I say. Chopping tomatoes and cheese in the kitchen, I can't help but hum.

"There. Better," he interrupts, coming down the steps from the bathroom fifteen minutes later. He has changed into another tailored black shirt, sleeves rolled up to the elbow.

"I've made something to eat. Let's go take a seat," I tell him, handing him a plate, and leading the way to the lounge. We eat, shoulder to shoulder, cross-legged on the sofa.

"Thanks for the food," he says, "I needed that." Placing down his plate on the coffee table, he scrutinises my face. "Ready for this?"

"Shoot."

"Andres was reluctant to meet at first, but I think he was intrigued to meet the man who helped bring his operation down. He spent some time sizing me up. A real prison thug. I explained what I knew of his links to the mafia, his known associates and how he got into the business. Then we got onto his earlier arrest. He wouldn't talk about the escape, but he said something intriguing."

"How so?"

"He seemed to think someone had killed his wife. Even mentioned Tío. Said the man seemed obsessed with Marianne."

"That's weird. So, *he* thinks my mother is dead?"

"Apparently."

"Did he say anything else?"

"Only that Tío had served in the French Army, and that the man was a Moroccan."

That was certainly a bit of a coincidence. "Did he say anything else?"

"No, but after he mentioned Tío, I had a brainwave."

"Yes?"

Leandro explained that he had contacted the nuns who cared for my uncle Jean on his deathbed.

"How?" I asked.

"It pays to speak Portuguese," he winked. "One of the nuns couriered Jean's diary. Did you know he was gay?"

"No, but that explains a lot."

"Apparently, the French police beat his boyfriend Rashid to death."

"But that's horrific!"

"Yes. I'm not sure what the police found more abhorrent really. Their homosexuality or the fact Rashid was a Moroccan kid. I mean, technically, he was the victim."

"What do you mean?"

"The age of sexual consent for homosexuals was twenty-one. Had they applied the law, Jean would have been jailed for molesting a young boy. I'm guessing your grandmother paid the policemen to take Rashid away and charge him with some spurious crime. The gardener's son and all that."

"Why did they murder him, then?" Charlotte asked.

"Things must have got out of control. Overzealous policemen. Institutional racism. You get the picture … And your grandmother, well, she was trying to protect the family name."

"How can you say that? It is barbaric."

Leandro shrugged. "Different times I suppose. I rang a colleague who tracked down the records. The police report said that Rashid had been caught stealing at your grandparents' house. Your mother Marianne was listed as witness in the deposition."

"You mean that she was there?" Charlotte felt her stomach tighten. "And you think someone was after her? But why not go after Jean? He was there too."

"I'm not sure. Helene must have arranged for Jean's name to be kept out of the record in case anyone had suspicions. The paperwork I found only mentions the theft of a necklace by a local boy."

"And Bonne-Maman sent Jean into exile?"

"That very day."

"This is insane."

"You must remember that those were very different times. Homosexuality was, you know ... and Morocco was ... In his diary, Jean mentions that it is Elizabeth who called the police. That's also important."

I think about Wilson. About the friendship my mother and Wilson shared. About the way she stood up against the bigots in Paris. I remember another incident. Aunt Elizabeth visiting, being very critical of Wilson's presence and of my mother's familiarity towards him.

It was my birthday. I could see it now as if I were back there. Jean had sent a notebook. A travel journal my mother had called it. It had unnerved Bonne-Maman.

From the other side of the sofa, Leandro is scrutinising my face. "Are you alright?"

Something has dawned on me. "My god, no wonder Jean lived like a recluse. The guilt ... How could they've done such a thing?"

"Those attitudes have always existed."

Leandro

After the conference, Leandro decided not to return to Brazil straight away. He joined me in Cardiff. We weren't prepared to say goodbye. And curious to see where this relationship could lead. I took time off from my translation job to show Leandro the sights. Together, we took a tour of Cardiff Castle and learnt about the architect, Burgess, and about Lord Bute. I showed him the Cardiff Bay development, explaining it stood where dockers had once loaded ships with black gold. I ambled along the St Fagans Museum of Welsh Life, soothed by its air of quiet stillness. Leandro said he understood the naive appeal Wales held for me, a place England had historically treated like a colony, yet which had benefited greatly from the Empire. He told me he too recognised himself in the inherent contradiction, that growing up mixed-race in Brazil, those paradoxes had been everywhere, tied to his ambiguous looks. "Now that I am in Wales, people see me two-dimensionally: foreign and Black," he added. I guess in a way we were united by the status of 'outsider' others had placed upon us.

Time passed. We started to look for a place of our own. Somewhere we could build a life together. On weekends, we would visit a number of satellite towns to Cardiff, guided by the listing of a family-run estate agent. After a few weeks, we spotted an apartment in a quiet town named Penarth.

"*Pen-arth*. It means the bear's head in Welsh," I said, reading from an information leaflet. "It is a sign, I know it."

Leandro arranged a viewing for the following Saturday. When the day arrived, we travelled early, eager to take stock of the area. The town hung on a clifftop overlooking the sea. To the east, the view swallowed the entirety of Cardiff Bay. The Severn Bridge which connected Wales to England, was faintly visible in the distance.

"You look pensive, Charlotte. What is it?" Leandro asked, holding my hand.

"If I squint, I can distinguish the location of my former flat," I said, pointing somewhere in the Bay. "And there, I almost drowned, once." With a finger, I traced the length of the Valleys which shoehorned Cardiff to the North, joined together by two waterways, the Ely and the Taff. At the foot of the hill was a marina, where Penarth Docks once stood, a focal point between Penarth and Grangetown. "This is where I lived after coming out of hospital," I showed him. Leandro stood quietly by my side for a while.

"Time to go," he finally said. We walked to the town centre, where we were met by the agent outside a rooftop flat overlooking a large square planted with a multitude of trees. Yew. Oak. Fir. Cypress. Juniper. Pine. Birch. Maple. Rowan. Chestnut. Poplar. Holly. Beech. Laurel. Cherry. Some local. Some brought by boat by amateur botanists in the nineteenth century. Some planted more recently by the council to encourage reforestation. The agent extolled the virtues of the area. The calm neighbourhood. The proximity to Cardiff. The apartment itself had a blue kitchen opening onto a well-lit living room and two bedrooms. Space for an office or for a child's bedroom, the agent added.

"What do you think?" Leandro asked once we were alone.

"It's perfect," I replied.

And close enough to work, he added. He had secured a post with the Institute of Welsh Affairs' magazine, writing long-form about international affairs. He pulled a little mobile phone out of his pocket and pressed the dial back. "We'll take it," he told the agent when she picked up. He planted a kiss on the top of my head. "We're going to be good here, Charlotte. Our first home together."

Penarth

Penarth was an affluent suburb, famous for its many gardens by the sea. We moved into the apartment in spring. The first evening, Leandro and I strolled about town, hand-in-hand, turning in front of the public library towards the sea, entering Alexandra Park with its neat, colourful borders and rows of blooming plum trees. Circling the cenotaph, a tall obelisk engraved with the names of local lads fallen in successive wars, we found a hidden set of steps. Leandro turned to look at me. "Shall we?" he said, gently tugging at my hand. I followed him down towards a large rectangular cage bordered by a hedgerow of thick hawthorns, dressed in bright-pink blossoms.

"What do you think this is?" I asked, intrigued.

Leandro drew closer, his eyes peering into the darkness. "Look," he pointed at a dash of sharp green. "And another one!"

I saw hints of lavender blue, sunshine yellow. "What are these?"

"Parakeets. We have them back in Brazil too. This is an aviary," he added with the exuberance of a happy child.

We stood side by side watching the birds perched on bamboo sticks, in pairs, trilling elaborate sounds at one another.

"They need each other. My mother used to say that a single parakeet will die of a broken heart." He wrapped his arms around me and whispered: "Will you be my parakeet?"

I could feel the thumping of his heart, so hard I thought I could hear it. I interlaced my fingers with his and laid back against his chest. "I love you, Leandro."

He buried his face into my neck, and we stayed for a while, nested into each other's space, watching the exotic birds fluttering about their cage.

"It's cruel to have them trapped like that," I said, after a while, repressing the urge to break the side door and release the birds.

"Shuuuut," Leandro blew into my ear, as if taming a wild animal. "We are ok, Charlotte. We are together."

The next morning, I rose, leaving Leandro asleep in our bed, and sat by the window in the living room, listening to the chorus of birds in the trees opposite. On a clear day I could see England in the distance, sometimes shaded off by the morning fog. I heard the shriek of the gulls and the roaming sound of waves crashing onto the pebble beach below. When the early morning swimmers started to dissipate, I walked up the hill into town. In Windsor Arcade, I purchased a handful of newspapers, a bag of oranges, two sausages, and a few streaks of bacon. I greeted faces that had become familiar. A world of morning strollers. Elegant Hat Lady, a retired midwife originally from Barbados who had once won an Olympic medal. Clive, a bold policeman walking his gruff-looking dog before his first shift. Always dressed in blue shorts and a rain jacket. Always smiling. Tippy-tap lady, a middle-aged mother of three who got into running to lose the baby weight. Hazel and Suleiman, the town green fingers who cared for the local community garden. An eclectic family who had welcomed us, the translator and the journalist, with open arms.

Nourished by their warmth, I returned home to our blue kitchen. Armed with a little tray, I called softly from the bedroom door. Leandro. He stirred and stretched like a cat, whilst I pulled the yellow curtains open and came to rest on the thick covers next to him, wrapping my legs over his.

"Good morning, sunshine," I whispered, scanning the lines of his face. "Did you sleep well?"

It had taken him time to adjust to the time difference, his sleep broken by vivid nightmares of a girl calling out his name, Clara.

"Why do you think she is coming to you now?"

"I don't know. Maybe on some level I feel guilty?"

"Guilty to be alive?"

"Guilty to be happy. To have a life, here, with you."

He reached forward and cupped my face. His fingers warm, comforting, safe. He pulled me closer. I rolled towards him and landed in the middle of the bed, upright, cross-legged. "Breakfast is served," I announced, leaning to grab the tray I had placed on the floor.

"Later," he said, lifting his head close. He pressed his lips on my forehead, my cheeks, brushed softly against my lips.

We made love unhurriedly, tracing each other's body, two people with all the time in the world. Afterwards, he held me, gently, searching deep into my eyes, singing a *saudade* in low, rumbling tones. Piece by piece his love, like the song, filled old crevices, expanding into the home we had made for ourselves.

Leandro wanted to memorise Wales, he said. To draw places in his mind, to anchor himself. To anchor us. Together, we visited the birthplace of Wales's patron saint – David. Dewi. In St Non we found the ruined cottage where his mother had reportedly been born. A place of pilgrimage, we read in a guide book. On the hedge between two fields was a little statue swallowed in brambles, coloured by the offerings invisible hands had tied.

Afterwards, we walked down to White Sands beach for a picnic. It was early June, the immaculate sand only interrupted by large black rocks and the regular cycle of tides. I felt like we were the only two people on earth.

"Could you live in a place like this?" I asked. As I did, I picked up a handful of sand and filled up my coat pockets.

I told him about the Welsh word for longing, *hiraeth*. It reminded him of the Portuguese word *saudade*. I recalled an anecdote I had read in a guidebook, many years before. Something about a local guy selling Welsh earth in a bottle to homesick Welsh expats in Australia.

"Do you believe this?" he asked me. "That we are tied to a land."

I thought about it. "You're my home. Not a place, or a time." I said after a while.

He scooped me up. "Where you go, I go," and he kissed the top of my head.

We walked back up the rural lane to the little cottage on the edge of St Davids where we were spending the night. For dinner, we grabbed two curried pasties from a local deli and ate them on the steps of the white cathedral, watching a black sheep graze between the gravestones. As the night drew in, we stopped at the Italian ice cream parlour and bought a tub, ginger and honey, which we shared. Meandering back to the cottage, we exchanged smiles with anonymous evening strollers, before retiring into the holiday let. There, I watched as Leandro built a fire inside a little wood burner, lighting a match, checking the ventilation, giving me a satisfied nod, before taking his place on the sofa by my side. I curled up into a ball, resting my head on his lap. This was the safest place in the world.

Elsewhere, a vote was taking place. One neither of us had a voice in. One that would change everything. After the results were publicised, a neighbour back in Penarth stopped me in the street.

"Will you be going home, now?" she asked.

I saw no malice in her question. More a mixture of curiosity and concern. Still, I felt fire in the pit of my stomach. "What's it to you?" I replied, harshly.

"I was just asking," she said, shrugging.

Brexit

After the Brexit vote, I launched into the task of applying for British Citizenship, driven by a sense of urgency. Leandro hadn't been in the UK long enough to meet the new residency status. His only chance was if he became my dependant.

The process of applying for citizenship was an administrative steeplechase. Despite almost twenty years in the UK, I had to take a test to demonstrate my ability to speak conversational English. The letter arrived, inviting me to attend an appointment the following Saturday in a local college. When I arrived, I noticed the Home Office banners in the lobby of the modern building, and the official-looking woman wearing a prominent name badge. She led me to a room on the first floor where I was asked to present my French passport and copy of the letter.

"Put your bag in this locker," she directed me. "No personal belongings in the room."

I nodded, relinquished my bag, and took the little key she handed me before escorting me to a waiting area.

"Room two," she said. "Wait here. You'll be called."

There were two other people waiting. Instinctively, all three of us avoided making eye contact. The man sported a mullet, and slightly outdated clothes. Eastern Europe, I guessed in this generic way you classified the places you hadn't visited. The woman, with her dark hair and designer glasses was Italian, beyond the shadow of a doubt. I wondered if they were also playing guess the nationality and what features would give me away as French. The door to room number two opened onto a sniffling middle-aged woman wrapped in a tartan shawl, reading glasses perched on the end of her nose.

"Charlotte ... how do you pronounce your last name?" she said, waving at her clipboard.

"Here," I told her, standing up, "Charlotte is fine."

She gestured for me to step into the room without further civilities, dabbing her red nose with a tissue crumpled in her left hand.

We sat opposite one another in an otherwise deserted classroom. She checked my details once more, then instructed me to describe my last holiday to her. "In English," she specified. I bristled, reminding myself why I was there. Breathe. I launched into a retelling of our recent trip to St Davids. She interrupted twice, asking for a detail here, a clarification there, noting something in her clipboard.

"That's enough," she concluded, raising her palm to silence me. "You can go."

I had stopped mid-sentence, and for a moment I felt dismissed. "Is that it?" I asked.

"Yes. Yes, go."

Two weeks later, it was the turn of the British Citizenship Test. The instructions said to travel to a test centre based in Newport. When I re-checked the address on the letter, I was assailed by doubts. No modern building here, just a shabby shop. The sign on the door informed me it was a driving school. I pushed the glass door, only to find it shut. Uncertain, I knocked, gently at first, then a little harder. A gentleman in a moth-eaten brown jumper appeared with a set of keys and let me in.

"Home Office Test?" he enquired, ascending a narrow staircase before I could answer.

At the top of the stairs was a tiny office with barred windows. "Take a seat a moment," he said, showing me a dusty old chair. "Do you have the letter?"

I handed it with my passport.

"Hold on to that a second," he said, pushing the passport back towards me.

I watched as he transcribed information from the letter to his computer screen for what felt like an eternity. The room was dusty and suffocating. I doubted anyone had cleaned the brown lacquered desk in years. Behind the man, so close I wondered whether they might fall and bury him, stood rows and rows of dirty folders marked with faded dates. Driving test paperwork, I assumed.

"Passport," he barked, startling me.

I complied, then sat motionless, eyes focused on a piece of blue tack on the edge of the desk whilst he entered yet more details onto the computer.

"I don't know why they make people like you take the test," he concluded eventually, handing me both passport and letter.

I wanted to ask what he meant by 'people like me' but thought better of it. I didn't want to spend another minute here with him. There was something intimidating about this man, as if he might snap at any time. Briskly, he stood, circled the brown desk and came level with my chair. He paused for a moment, as if he were considering something, then carried on towards the corridor.

"This way," he called from another room.

The corridor opened onto a long and narrow room. To my surprise, I discovered lines of people sat in complete silence in front of computer screens encased in individual little grey booths.

"This is you," the man said, pointing at an empty spot.

I pulled the office chair, cringing at the loud squeaking noise, and sat in front of the online test.

"Just press the start button on the screen when you're ready. It is fairly intuitive."

He left and I remained in this strange room, feeling alone amidst dozens of strangers. Better get to it, I thought, checking my watch. I shook the mouse and the little arrow on the screen hovered over the large rectangle marked START. The first question materialised in bold letters on the screen. Four possible answers. A click to select my answer, another click to press NEXT, and so on until I reached THE END. I checked my watch again. Forty-six seconds. It took me forty-six seconds to complete the test with its patronising questions. I looked around. Nobody else had moved. I pushed my chair back, stood and moved towards the exit. Outside, a cloud of cigarette smoke hit me. I took a deep inhale.

"It was hard, wasn't it?" a nervous little woman spoke. She looked Middle Eastern. Syrian maybe.

"Sure," I said, feeling a sudden kinship with this stranger. I recalled the man's comment in the office. *People like me.* People with the right sort of passport is what he had meant. For me, however frustrating the process had been, it was little more than a rubber-stamping exercise. I knew that if it had been Leandro standing here instead of me, our prospects would be very different. Less certain. I took hold of the woman's hand. "Good luck," I told her, offering her a smile.

As expected, I passed. A hefty bill later, I stood at the Barry Registry Office for the obligatory citizenship ceremony. The room was small, stuffy, filled with discarded folders piled high in one corner. The Registrar placed a little Union Jack on her desk. "Here we are," she said, handing me the script I was expected to read in order to swear allegiance to the Queen and her descendants. None of my Welsh friends would ever agree to do that, I thought. The assistant recorded my reading on a little camera. "For posterity," she said, whilst the Registrar circled her desk to shake my hand and transmit the certificate which confirmed my new status. "I'm afraid we've run out of the English leaflet, but here is the Welsh version. We have a stack of those," she told me, rolling her eyes.

Uncertain what reaction she was expecting from me, I remained silent and offered a restrained smile. Behind her, Leandro was giving me the thumbs up. I repressed the urge to giggle. She turned towards him. "You must feel so proud," she said, without a hint of irony.

On the way out, we walked back to the main desk and booked our wedding date.

Ynys Echni

The wedding took place in Ynys Echni's lighthouse under the competent gaze of the same woman Registrar. The space was small and circular, the whitewashed walls contrasting with a black and white tiled floor. Leandro stood in the centre of a room lit from above. He turned towards the door, where Max waited. I stepped from behind him and took his arm. Max was tall, even by American standards. Despite his advanced age, his presence was imposing. We both stood side by side for a moment. In the distance I noticed Leandro scrutinising my face. Looking for any sign of doubt, I thought. This wasn't how he had wanted to do things. Circumstances had forced us to act with haste. His eyes found mine, his mind convinced for a moment he saw hesitation in my gaze, but no. Finally, he saw it. My wide smile.

"Shall we?" Max bellowed.

I nodded, taking a step forward.

Afterwards, the little delegation boarded a boat which chartered us back to the barrage.

"No time to waste," the captain explained. "We have to catch the tide." Five miles off the coast of Cardiff – Ynys Echni was a symbolic space sat in the Bristol channel. In between two nations, like a life raft. A place of less than a square mile that seemed to echo our situation. Filled with seabirds and slowworms, it had once been the location of a religious retreat centre, then a sanctuary for cholera sufferers. Now it was deserted of human occupants, providing the perfect home for a colony of protected migrating birds.

The reception was held in the Makers Guild, a rectangular glass building dropped on a concrete island between two main roads, Bute Street and Lloyd George Avenue; one axis running across old Butetown, the other marking the edge of the redeveloped part of the Bay. We were joined by a handful of acquaintances, work friends, and neighbours. Health had prevented Leandro's mother from joining us from Brazil. My mother also was absent, on a cruise somewhere in the Mediterranean. The wedding plans had been rushed, gripped as we were by the fear of being separated. Still, there was meaning in the ceremony that had taken place that morning. Our union like an island, witnessed by Max, its lighthouse-keeper.

Cardiff Bay

"Can I ask you something?" Leandro approached Max, handing him a champagne flute. They stood on the edge, observing as Charlotte led a group of guests onto the dance floor.

"Ynys Echni – Flat Holm. Did you know it is from there that Marconi sent the first ever radio signal across the Atlantic? A fitting place for your union," Max commented, as if to himself.

Leandro was taken aback. "I ... yes, I think I read this in the brochure."

"Forgive me. You had a question," Max said, an inscrutable expression bringing life to his wrinkled face.

"I've been wondering ... Why did you send the box?"

"Ah, the box. I'd rather hear your theories. You must have theories, Leandro? I hear you're a tenacious investigative journalist."

Leandro wondered if Max was testing him or if this was an old spy habit, to unsettle the adversary. "I keep going back to the laptop," Leandro replied. "You see, we start asking questions, and shortly after Charlotte's place gets broken into."

"It happens."

"See, that's the thing ... It does ... happen ... but all they took was the laptop and her notebook. A very targeted burglary, wouldn't you say?"

"I suppose. And what do you make of that?"

"The Head of the SDECE sent Francis to rescue his cousin by marriage. A covert operation, under pretence of cross-agency collaboration. The more I think about it though, the less that makes sense. To get rid of Andres, all he needed was to have him arrested. Marianne would have been free from him. There had to be more. Something else. Something that touched him more closely."

"I take it you have another theory?"

"Nobody went after Andres when he escaped because it wasn't about him. When I visited him in prison, Andres told me he thought his wife had been killed by his business partner, Tío."

Max raised an eyebrow. "Go on."

"She disappears and so does he. A rational conclusion would have been that his partner had double-crossed him and ran off with his wife. Instead, Andres believes the man murdered his wife. He said Tío had a strange obsession with her."

"So, all this time Andres believed Marianne was dead?"

"See, I think it was Tío all along who worried Elizabeth's husband."

"Keep going."

"You told Charlotte that Tío was from Rabat. A bit of a coincidence. After reading Jean's diary, I checked the police record about Rashid's death. I believe Charlotte told you about that."

Max nodded.

"The report mentions two young women without naming them, however there was an address."

"And?"

"If someone had bothered to look, gone to the house even, maybe spoken to the cook? Maybe this person would have found out Marianne had left for Europe a few days after Rashid's death. The behaviour of a guilty person, maybe? Someone working from the police report alone would have been unable to piece together the exact circumstances of Rashid's death. All they would have known was that the boy died in a French home, for an alleged theft witnessed by two young women, one of whom had fled the country shortly after. Maybe they would have wanted to *speak* to Marianne, believing her to be responsible for the death?"

"Ok, so the Head of the SDECE did all this to protect Marianne?"

"I think he wanted to identify and neutralise the man who presented a threat to his wife, Elizabeth, Marianne's cousin, and by extension his career."

"And you think Tío was that man? An interesting hypothesis."

"Don't take me for a fool, Max. He was one of your undercover agents."

"It was a long time ago."

"It was. And a man like yourself does not forget. That's why you sent the box, I think. Who was he, Max?"

"Alright young man. Very tenacious indeed. His name was Lieutenant Abdel Ben Idris, originally from Rabat, celibate. His only known family was a sister to whom he sent half of his pay. The man I knew was a model of rectitude, dedicated to his widowed sister. I think her name was Soumia. It was terrible what happened to her boy."

Something clicked. "Rashid? Lieutenant Idris's nephew was Rashid?"

Max nodded.

"My god. What about Marianne? Obviously, she would have known?"

"I doubt it. Marianne met him in Colombia. Even if she'd realised that he was Moroccan, she had no way of making the connection. To her, Tío was one of her husband's acolytes."

"And you never told her?"

"I saw no need. Francis and Marianne embraced the fiction. They had new papers. A new name. Besides, Idris had disappeared, and we had no reason to believe he would pursue the matter further."

"We?"

Emerging from the group of dancers at that moment, Charlotte handed Leandro a large knife. "There you are, husband of mine. Time to cut the wedding cake."

"Sure," he gripped the handle. "Max? Will you join us?"

Max effaced himself, gesturing for Leandro to walk on ahead.

"We're not done," Leandro murmured over his shoulder.

In response Max raised his glass, "To the bride and groom."

"To the bride and groom," the room of guests echoed.

Max remained in the periphery for the rest of the night, observing. He recalled receiving the news of the break-in. Someone from the old team was keeping tabs on old cases. No doubt they would have

207

been unnerved by an investigative journalist poking around, asking about Tío. Since the SDECE had been replaced by a new agency and its former boss was long dead, Max had believed it would be safe for Charlotte to learn the truth. He had had second thoughts when she had turned up on his doorstep in London, with a gash on her head. Sloppy work, he'd thought. Someone had been panicking about the possible embarrassment in case Armand's abuses of power were uncovered. France was already struggling to articulate its colonial past. They didn't need a scandal. But then, nothing. Whatever Charlotte had recorded on her laptop had not warranted further actions. And since there had not been further incidents, Max had concluded that whoever had orchestrated the break-in no longer saw the couple as a potential risk.

Maracaibo

"What are we doing here?" Marianne whispered to Francis, a hint of suspicion in her voice.

"There is a fishing boat waiting for us," he replied, pointing at a small rusty boat docked on the far corner of the harbour, half hidden under a veil of blue and green fishing nets. Francis parked the car, handing the bag to Marianne.

"Let's go. Grab this. I brought you a change of clothes."

Before Marianne opened the passenger door, she stared at the silver band on her ring finger, took it off, opened her handbag and placed the wedding ring in a handkerchief that also contained the silver pendant Francis had sent as a sign, and a picture of Andres and her in Avianca uniforms, a reminder not to be so naive in the future. Closing her bag, she followed Francis to a trawler. "Max, come give us a hand," Francis called out.

A lanky man emerged from the cabin, dressed in black trousers and a beige shirt. He held himself straight, straighter than a fisherman would, Marianne thought. He leaped over the banister, athletic, landing on the plank that connected the little boat to the pontoon.

"Max, meet Marianne. Marianne, Max."

"Now let's get going," Max replied in lieu of a greeting. "We want to catch the tide."

"Where are we going on this?" asked Marianne, unconvinced the rust-ridden boat could float.

"Fort-de-France. There is a military base there, Francis replied, "Now hop on."

"I don't understand," she said. "Why are we going to Martinique?"

"Martinique is a French overseas territory, Lady," Max explained, rubbing his neck.

Marianne gave him a confused look. Behind her, Francis laughed.

"I couldn't safely fly you to France from Colombia, so I decided to bring France a little bit closer," he said.

The crossing passed in a dream, Marianne sat in the hull, eyes closed, her body gently rocked by the lapping of waves, whilst from the deck the voices of Francis and Max intermingled in a reassuring baritone soundtrack.

"You are home," Max told her as they reached the pontoon. Martinique was French territory. Francis and her disembarked.

"*Bonne chance*," Max called, before sailing the rusty boat back towards Colombia.

Elizabeth's husband had commandeered a military aircraft which flew Marianne and Francis to the army port of Toulon, in the South of France. It was the first time Marianne had ever set foot on the soil of metropolitan France. She was thirty years old.

8. FRACTURE

Max

Leandro placed a bowl of soup on a small rectangular wooden tray and headed in the direction of Max's bedroom. "Why didn't you tell us you were ill?" he reproached the diminished old man, placing the tray on the covers.

"We would have come sooner," I added, stepping from the darkness.

Leandro and I had received a phone call from the housekeeper the night before, urging us to come at once. I was the only one of her employer's relatives the lady knew of, she had told Leandro, adding she had found the number in Mr Max's address book. It was Sunday; trains were few and far between. We would be along as soon as we could, Leandro had replied. We had thrown a few belongings in a rucksack and walked the six kilometres to Cardiff Central, down Penarth hill and across the orange pedestrian bridge to the International Sports Village. From there, we traced the length of the river Taff, mechanically marching side by side, parallel to Grangetown, without once uttering a word. At Central, the ticket booth was empty. I had gestured at the automated vending machines. The first one was out of service. The second came to life when Leandro tapped the touchscreen. He entered the destination. London. Two singles. Paid with a credit card. Ninety minutes later we boarded an empty coach, threw our bag on the top rack and sat down, shoulder to shoulder.

It was dark when we reached the apartment on Cavendish Street. The cleaner greeted us with a sigh of relief. "Mr Max is bad," she said in a whisper, as if trying to prevent him from hearing. "I prepared food in the kitchen for you. Make sure he has at least a few spoons of soup."

Afterwards, she unhooked her raincoat from the peg in the entrance, picked up her bag of cleaning products, dropped her set of keys on the little wooden table in the entrance hall, and closed the door, casting a final glance around at the home she had maintained for over two decades.

"I'll make tea," Leandro said, heading towards the kitchen.

I was grateful for the time he was giving me with Max.

I remembered the day my father had died. The journey to Paris. My father, laid out in his navy-blue suit, clean, waxy, cold. Already gone. I shook my head, looked around at the familiar objects in this London apartment that had been my home, my anchor, my salvation many times. Over the years, Max had been a friend, a confidant, a father. I pushed the door to his room and stepped in. The air smelt of a mixture of disinfectant, decay, and chicken broth. Clutching my jaw, I moved in the penumbra of half-drawn curtains towards the space occupied by a large double bed. A laboured purring emerged from under a heavy-looking tartan blanket, conjuring in my mind an indistinct need to run. "This isn't happening," I murmured, swallowing a sob. The blanket moved, revealing a bony hand. "Gwen?"

I took a deep breath. "It's me, Max, Charlotte."

"The old bat called you. I told her there was no need."

"Oh Max, look at you," my voice wavered.

Across the bed, Leandro stood with a clenched jaw as I presented a spoonful of soup to the man who, only a few months before, had seemed so intimidating. Max turned away in a gesture of refusal reminiscent of a stubborn toddler. The levelling effect of time. I discarded the tray, and patted Max's hand. My touch seemed to soothe him. "Not much time now, boy," he said, looking straight at Leandro, with an unwavering smile that contrasted with his weak tone.

"You never said why you sent the box?" Leandro said.

"Secrets are a funny thing," Max replied, his eyes scanning the darkness for some invisible ghost. "One moment they signify the difference between life or death; the next they're dusty scraps, relegated to the archives of time."

"What does that mean?" I asked, leaning forward. I clung to Max's hand now, pressing hard as if to urge him on.

214

"Dear Charlotte," Max called in a rasp. "You have to understand. The manner of that poor boy's death must have been incredibly traumatic for your mother. You know, the Rabat she grew up in was permissive. Post-war, it was a playground where she would have experienced the boundaries between the communities as fluid. You understand? What happened to Rashid, to Jean for that matter, it was shocking."

"So, she ran away, kept silent all this time? No. How could she?" I raised my voice.

"She was only a young girl, Charlotte. Sometimes you just move forward so as not to be swallowed by your past."

I nodded.

Max's chest rose heavily now. He turned towards Leandro. "There isn't much time," he said, gasping for air. "I want you to know ... I want you to know the truth." He paused, trying to find his breath. Leandro leant forward. Max whispered something in his ear, then patted him on the shoulder. "Take care of her for me, will you?"

I pressed the old man's hand against my face, swallowing back some tears. "I love you, Max," I murmured.

"That's why I sent the box," Max added. "He'll tell you. Then you can make peace with her."

"Who can make peace?" I asked turning from Max to Leandro, frowning.

"I'll explain later," Leandro replied.

"One more thing." Max picked up a brown envelope from his bedside table and handed it to Leandro.

Leandro and I sat, watching the rising and falling of Max's breath as it slowed, becoming imperceptible. Finally, it became still. We looked up then, staring into each other's eyes. Leandro reached across to my hand. "I've got you."

The envelope contained the notes Max had subtracted from the CIA's records, notes about Marianne's presence in Colombia, and instructions for his own funeral: The name of a solicitor; a number

215

to call to notify the Agency. Putting the envelope in his bag, Leandro picked up the receiver in the living room and dialled. An hour later, two men in dark suits knocked on the door. They boxed the content of the office, removing files, diaries, even the computer. Polite, they thanked us and left as they had come.

Turning towards the window, I sighed at the rain outside.

Clara

Following Max's death, Leandro told me everything he knew about Jean, Rashid, and Lieutenant Idris. I had questions for my mother now. Why she ran away? Why she never spoke about any of this? Questions I had been afraid to ask. She pressed us to visit her in Paris, but we were soon forced to put our plans on hold. The prospect of Brexit had made us weary of travelling out of Britain until Leandro's situation was regularised, in case he wasn't allowed back in. Meanwhile, we refurbished the flat in Penarth with money Max had kindly willed us.

Clara was born six months after the funeral, pulling us into the whirlwind that comes with a new-born baby. Nappies. Feeds. Sleepless nights. Most of all, Clara was like a beacon of hope for both of us. The certainty that no matter what civil servants concluded about Leandro's right to remain, we were a family.

My mother was excited, of course, at the prospect of her first grandchild. She visited with increasing regularity over the first three years, bringing tokens from France in the form of jam jars, wine bottles, and children's picture books. In that time, it never seemed right to mention the past, enthused as we were by Clara's first bath, first tooth, first steps.

Then almost as soon as Leandro's papers came through, the global pandemic spread, closing all borders in its wake. Cut off from my mother, and from pretty much everyone else, Leandro and I grew increasingly insular, as if the world had shrunk to this single unit: an apartment in Penarth, the place where our daughter grew, shaped entirely by the stories we told and the songs of birds coming through the window.

Return

A jackdaw's hard repetitive 'tchack' cuts through the clattering wings of the pigeons standing sentinel on our Penarth rooftop. They await the seeds the downstairs neighbour scatters on her birdfeeder each morning. Then the heavy birds take flight, my cue to get up also. Our apartment is surrounded by trees, like an island amid a sea of green canopies. From here, the low murmur of urban life is muted, made less relevant by the chromatic passing of seasons and the routines of woodpeckers, blue tits, bats, and squirrels. Quite a contrast with the revving of traffic from my childhood. Every morning at six I used to wake to the high-pitched screech of the municipal bin lorry's lifting mechanism as it tilted the multitude of wheelie bins that stood in front of the large Haussmann buildings. I heard the concierge swearing as he dragged the bins back through the service entrance, hard plastic thudding against the paved alleyway, the clanking of keys absorbed by the reinforced steel door which he shut behind him. I would rise then, knowing my mother would be preparing breakfast while my father shaved. Both filling the apartment with the scents of my childhood: sandalwood, freshly baked bread, and ground coffee.

Today, Clara and I will travel back in time, catching the Penarth train to Cardiff Central, onto the London train to Paddington, and from there to St Pancras International where the Eurostar will carry us to Paris. A twelve-hour journey from Wales to Paris, her first one. I lay down two plates on the kitchen counter, pour us breakfast tea with a splash of milk and butter two slices of bread before smothering them in Marmite. In the background, the radio is reporting on some evacuation. Clara emerges from her bedroom fully dressed, eager for the adventure to commence. We eat our toast and drink our brew hurriedly, grab our bags and lock the front door without as much as a glance back.

"This was a present from your grandmother. I think she's been everywhere with this thing," I tell her, lifting a wheeled blue case and carrying it down the stairs. I place my charge onto the ground outside and gently pat it as you might a faithful companion. For a second, I think about Arthur. Clara climbs on the blue beast's back and I pull them both along in the direction of the station. The pavement around our place is distorted by tree roots. The case hits every ridge and crack, rumbling loudly, sending spooked jackdaws into flight, like a procession. There, a mould-green Arriva two-coach train rests on the track, an old relic that should have been replaced as part of the electrification of the line, on reprieve because of the delays caused by the pandemic. I hand Clara her mask and we both step into an empty carriage, faces covered. Earlier, a train operator interviewed on the radio had lamented that only sixty per cent of passengers have returned. It's a step back for sustainable travel, he said. On every news outlet the climate crisis has been overshadowed by daily counts: of new positive tests, new patients in intensive care, new deaths. For years now, the news has been filled with figures: 20,000 refugees from Afghanistan brought to the UK, families airlifted to the UK from Kabul airport, supported by armed eighteen-year-old soldiers juggling guns with babies. Leandro is somewhere amongst them, reporting. I worry.

At Cardiff Central, the London train is thirty minutes late. We sit and stare at the station clock, wishing for no further delays. "Will we make it?" Clara asks, leaning into my shoulder.

"I think so," I reply, my voice muffled by folds of cotton. I count the spare minutes on my fingers over and over again, as if doing so could somehow bend time. I hear my mother's voice telling me that we should have flown instead. The Tannoy comes to life, apologising for a further thirty-five-minute delay. "Will we make it now?"

"I don't know," I say, my reply swallowed up by a distorted platform announcement in Welsh, repeating in English. I feel the weight of doubt pressing against my chest. Maybe this journey is a mistake. The Tannoy shrieks to life once more, words unintelligible.

"What did it say?" I ask.

"Something about further delay," Clara replies.

"The London train is always late," I shrug. "We'll be alright."

So now we wait, for the Swansea train to arrive and carry us to London, for the Hammersmith and City line to transport us to the Eurostar departure lounge, for the border patrols to confirm we have the right documentation to clear customs: a sworn statement for the French government to confirm we are symptom-free, proof of vaccination for me, a negative test of less than twenty-four hours for my daughter. The officer behind the glass panel orders us to remove our masks so he can confirm our identity. The motion calls fragments of images into my mind: a veiled woman uncovering her face at Istanbul airport many years before; the piercing green eyes of an Afghan girl captured in 1984 by Steve McCurry for the cover of *National Geographic* – a haunting gaze that remained on the wall of my childhood bedroom until I left Paris. I wonder now what she thought of the multitude of Western eyes staring at her image in books and museums, whilst her country burnt. Still, I pray Leandro is safe.

I'm pulled back by the heavy thump of the French official stamping our passports.

"Look, you've got a stamp!" I show Clara, trying to sound jovial. Inwardly, I cringe at the first concrete sign of what until now has been an abstract change.

At Paris-Gare du Nord the tall caryatids in white stone monitor our arrival. My mother is standing on the main concourse, straight as a marble statue, face hidden behind a surgical mask. We huddle, unsure whether to hug after months of social isolation.

"I brought the car," she says, dragging Clara by the hand. I try to keep up, yanking the blue suitcase behind me. I'm no longer aware of the noise the case makes amid the hum of city traffic. Looking ahead I notice, just before they disappear into the car, that grandmother and daughter have the same walk.

Soon we reach the Opera Garnier, a work commissioned by Napoleon III in his own honour, and filled with the technical innovations of the time. A few minutes later, the church of La Madeleine, originally built to commemorate Napoleon I's great army, stands before us, its colonnades encased in scaffolding. Then we're alongside the golden-tipped obelisk that's proudly anchored in the middle of the Place de la Concorde. To our right, the Champs-Élysées, lined by rows of imposing horse chestnuts, shrink towards the Arc de Triomphe and the flame of the Unknown Soldier. To our left is the Orangerie, a small, glass-panelled museum flanked by the Seine and the rue de Rivoli. My mother and I point out these familiar buildings to Clara, as I realise for the first time how many of the capital's tourist landmarks are linked to France's history of colonial expansion. Ahead of us, across the river, I point towards the National Assembly.

"It looks like a Greek temple!" Clara exclaims.

"Yes. Culture is a patchwork," my mother replies. "In France's case, there have been many influences."

I think about the way architecture reflects those unspoken influences my mother is referring to. Everywhere, Paris is fighting to retain its air of empire.

Eventually, we reach our destination, an apartment block on the western edge of the city. My mother presses a button and manoeuvres her car between two imposing automatic gates and into an underground carpark. "It's very dark," Clara remarks, blinking in the automatic lighting which meets us as we descend into darkness.

This is not the place of my childhood. After my father passed, my mother moved to a smaller apartment, one I have never seen. She parks the car and leads us out, through a series of locked doors. "There is the lift." She points to a sliding panel. Inside, floor-to-ceiling mirrors fail to relieve the claustrophobia of the little cage. I never liked lifts.

Clara is excited by the novelty and presses every button before my mother and I can object. We ride up like mackerel in a tin, the door opening and closing on each floor. "It all looks the same," she says. She's right. We catch glimpses of corridors painted a peach colour, of doors trimmed in sage green, of large brass handles. We follow my mother as she steps out on what she tells us is her floor. Large, tinted mirrors capture the electric light, sending back a warm glow across the marble tiles. Next to each door, a small plaque is etched with the name of its owner. My mother pulls a key from her handbag and unlocks the second door on the left. I hold my breath as the door opens onto this unknown place.

Living in a foreign country all my adult life, I have often wondered what makes a house a home. As I step into the apartment, I am assailed by smells from childhood – *ras el hanout* from the kitchen, my mother's citronella perfume in the bathroom, the faint scent of dark tobacco emanating from familiar furniture. The apartment is smaller, lighter, laid out differently, but within its walls my mother has recreated my childhood home. Here, each carpet, each table, each chair has a place in my memory. The decorative objects which signify moments from my parents' lives are all around us. While my mother gives her granddaughter a tour of the apartment, I sit in the oddly familiar living room as if for the hundredth time.

Memories

On day two, we take the bus to the Esplanade du Trocadero. Disappointingly, it is hidden from view by large opaque plastic sheeting behind which builders work to pressure-wash the stone buildings back to white. Outside, Black street vendors tout miniature replicas of the Eiffel Tower. I smile at this constant from my childhood.

"I thought we could be visitors for a day," my mother suggests, pointing at an open-top bus decorated with a big vinyl-wrapped tower. We climb the winding staircase, find a seat. A man hands us a pair of cheap earphones.

"This is the place where the guillotine stood during the French Revolution," I tell Clara. "You know, chop, chop." I make a slicing movement with the edge of my hand.

"Gross," Clara replies, sticking her tongue out.

For two hours we hop from landmark to landmark, performing what must look like an exercise in oral tradition. In reality, all we are transferring are borrowed memories.

By day three Clara has integrated, making the little room adjacent to the kitchen her own. On waking, she pulls the blue curtains with Provencal patterns that once decorated my childhood room, opens the window, and steps onto the white tiled balcony, inhaling the scent of flowers my mother has planted in large terracotta pots.

"What's that smell?" she asks when I join her.

I lean towards the red petals, the earthy fragrance filling my nostrils. For a moment, I am back inside a makeshift greenhouse in Châtellerault.

"Geraniums. They were my grandmother's favourite." I step back inside. "Help me set breakfast."

As we lay the table in the dining room, I consider this strange choice of flowers. Walking back onto the balcony where my mother is regaling in the morning sun, I launch into my enquiry.

"Did you ever forgive her, Mum?" I ask, pointing at the flowers.

"Forgive who?"

"Bonne-Maman. Your mother."

"What are you talking about?" she says, her quizzical eyebrow raised.

"Rabat. Jean. I know."

I had imagined that once she'd realised that I knew, my mother would feel vindicated, able to let go of what I assumed were decades of repressed emotions eating her up. Instead, she looks at me with total incomprehension. I pull the recent picture of Andres from my pocket, present it to her as a peace offering. "This is Andres now," I tell her.

"I don't care about the fate of that man," she spits out, her scorn palpable.

Undeterred, I articulate for her the connection between Andres and the man she knew as Tío. Between that man and a boy named Rashid. I guess at a slight shift in her outraged demeanour then. Her eyes, hard a moment ago, fill with tears.

"I never knew," she murmurs, pulling her hands into fists. "We wronged the poor boy. Destroyed so many lives," she hesitates, pensive. Then as if she remembered I was there, she repositions herself in the garden chair and pats the corner of her eyes with her index fingers. "It was a long time ago, Charlotte. What possessed you to go rummaging into my past like this?"

I'm having a déjà vu moment. At the same time, she looks shrunken somehow. Yet, I persist. "Did you never think about Rashid's mother over the years? About how you would have felt if it was your boy?"

Her face tightens. "You don't understand."

"Understand?"

"Those were different times."

"Bullshit. What is wrong now was wrong then."

"What do you want from me? This ..." She waves at the air between us, "... this is simply sordid. Your generation, always hunting for drama."

224

"Not drama. The truth. Don't you want to honour Rashid and your brother's memory with the truth?"

"What good would it do? They're dead. They're long dead. They're all dead. Should I wash my dirty laundry in public to make *you* feel better?"

At that moment, Clara decants onto the balcony. "There you are. Play with me, Granma." She pulls her grandmother to her feet and drags her to the living room table, where she has set up a game of snakes and ladders. Before stepping over the threshold, my mother turns back towards me. "Stop this nonsense, I beg you."

The Journal

Alone on the balcony, I feel my head buzzing. How could it have gone so wrong? Unsure what to do next, I reach for my day bag and pull out the object I found in a box marked 'Charlotte's bedroom' the day before. A tanned red leather notebook with encrusted golden lettering.

"It is from your uncle Jean."

"It is empty."

I open the journal, and thumb through notes from a childhood trip to Istanbul traced in large, uneven letters, and illustrated with doodles: a mosque in blue crayon, the swirl of a loaf of bread bought in the bazaar, a little brown bear. I pause on a fresh page. All those years ago, Jean sent the notebook for a reason. I start writing.

Over a few days, I scribble frantically, recording a detailed account of everything I know, everything I've learnt, everything I've experienced. In doing so, I crystallise what, until now, has been a moving story, down to Max's last confession to Leandro:

After Max had dropped my parents off in Martinique he had returned to Colombia. Grasping the risk Idris presented, he had tracked the lieutenant down for weeks, finally locating him in a motel a hundred miles from Cartagena. Max. Dear Max had confronted the man, urged him to stop. A fight had ensued. A punch. A fall. A cracked skull. Max had fled, leaving the body of the lieutenant behind.

Several decades had passed. Max, retired and weary, had thought to unburden himself. It was uncharacteristic for a former spook of course, but we were the closest thing to his family and maybe hearing from his old friend how much the relationship between my mother and I had deteriorated had made him unusually sentimental. We would never know for sure. He had revealed the death of Lieutenant Idris to my father over lunch, in a café overlooking Notre-Dame. My father, on hearing the true identity of Tío, had connected the dots. After all, he knew Jean and probably Rashid. Maybe he'd wondered about them, since he was trained to notice the sort of details others often missed. What had broken my father was the realisation of what had come after. The enormity of the cover-up orchestrated by the Head of the SDECE. The abuse of power of a man he had considered his mentor. The ramifications.

In Max's eyes, Idris had died so my parents could live a normal life. But to my father, Idris had been their victim. An uncle consumed by grief, wronged by corrupt French police officers, wronged by Marianne's family. He'd thought to confront his former boss who was still alive in those days. Shortly after, he'd been sectioned.

Where do the secrets end? I write.

In the apartment, my mother and I avoid each other, using Clara as our unsuspecting go-between. Then one night as I am putting the finishing touch to this strange family record, a thought occurs to me.

My mother is on her bed, reading.

"What happened to Wilson?" I ask.

Instead of an answer, she sighs.

"You never talk about him anymore."

"You never ask," she replies, the words heavy with blame. "You're too absorbed in the drama of your own existence. Children are like that, you'll see." She points her chin in the direction of Clara's room.

"Are the two of you still in touch? You used to write all the time. How old is he now? Fifty?"

"Fifty-four," she replies, with startling certainty.

"Fifty-four. Dear Wilson. How is he?"

Her exhale seems to last an eternity. Wedged between two pillows, she suddenly seems very small. "Did you know Wilson was a *Mahométan*?" she asks.

Wilson

Wilson underestimated the wave of paranoia that followed 9/11, especially amongst his colleagues. At night, once the girls had gone to bed, he whispered words in his wife's ears about the unnerved security staff ready to blow at the least breech of compliance; the line managers encouraging employees to make judgement calls about passengers based on the way people looked or sounded; the armed men and women who seemed to relish the sudden surge of power. Yet, Wilson would always conclude that they were only doing their job, maybe to reassure her. Maybe to reassure himself. It was a heavy burden, keeping everyone safe.

His wife met such faith in the system with a dose of reserve. "The police imagine threats everywhere," she told him. "You should see them on the metro. The way they stare at people. The way they stare at us. I'm scared, Wilson."

There was a raid. Early one morning. Wilson heard a noise and came down the stairs armed with a *casse-tête*, thinking they were being burgled. The *casse-tête* was a gift from his father. A memento from Nigeria.

Nicole heard a big shattering sound as the police broke down their front door. The rapid popping sound of guns. Reaching the bottom of the stairs with a terrorised child on each hip, she witnessed Wilson lying on the floor, screaming at them not to hurt the children.

There was a brief enquiry. The policeman who had opened fire was found to have acted within reason – proportional response, they called it, as if Wilson's wooden stick was a match to their guns. And Wilson ... well, he was a Muslim, working in a position of trust at the airport. Someone in the HR department had checked his record. Found some discrepancies. Reported Wilson to the Border Agency. Apparently, he had entered France illegally that first time.

228

His real passport had carried a fake visa. A transit visa to the United States. Every paper he had acquired after that was under false pretence. His residency invalid. His marriage annulled. A whole lifetime spent in France erased, just like that.

Wilson was deported back to Nigeria a month after the raid, having been detained in a centre for illegal migrants a few hundred metres from the office he had occupied at the airport all these years. A far-right paper reported on the event: 'Successful police raid. Muslim alien deported.' Nothing about a Frenchman, a loving husband, a father. Wilson's assimilation a faint veil, so easily torn.

Cultural Aphasia

"You loved him so much. I remember the two of you roller-skating in the park," my mother recalls, her voice unsteady.

"Why didn't you say?"

She shrugs.

"And Nicole?" I ask.

"Nigeria. She expatriated herself. They moved in with her in-laws. I spoke to her once. She doesn't want anything to do with France anymore. She said Wilson's spirit is broken."

I think about Leandro. About how easily Wilson's story could be our own.

Long after my mother goes to bed, I sit on the balcony and look up at the stars, thinking about my old childminder. Only now do I realise how cut off I have been. All the events I missed over the years. I long accepted missing relatives getting married. Children being baptised. These are happy events after all, and I can still rejoice from a distance. But what happened to Wilson ... In my mind, France is crystallised, frozen in that year of 2001 when I left. Or maybe before, even. Into a myth that only ever existed in the history books from my childhood. And now, here I am, in this city of my birth where memories collide with facts. The society I described to my daughter only a few days ago suddenly feels alien, made up.

Now, I notice new signs. On the radio the news presenter comments on the rise of the National Front. The papers are full of debates about the meaning of universal values when second and third generation migrants seem segregated in the *banlieues*. The language is polarising. Filled with new vocabulary. The word Frexit has entered presidential debates.

In one generation since her father, Marine Le Pen has successfully reframed a narrative of racism into an act of civic duty. Forgotten are the sins of the father, a soldier during the wars of Indochina and Algeria, a man who once described the Holocaust as a 'detail of history'. Forgotten all that we owe the people from the Maghreb who populate disenfranchised *banlieues* on the outskirts of Paris. My generation has been framed by the unspoken violence and torture our forebears inflicted.

"There's so many of *them*," my mother comments as we drive past a group of North African-looking men on our way to the theatre the next day. "They come here to find work, but we have no work to give them. Unemployment is already too high in France. We can't be responsible for everyone else's problems," she says, echoing the rising rhetoric.

I press my lips together and look away, searching for the right words along a pavement littered with sleeping bags. Once again, I think about Leandro, wish he could be with us now. I feel the need to gather my little family around, to huddle like penguins. From the back, Clara's voice pierces the silence. "Where are the men from, Granma?"

"I'm not sure, sweetheart. Morocco probably."

"Are you friends?"

"Now why would you ask that?"

"You're from Morocco too, aren't you?"

"I'm French. They're migrants."

Such finality. Suddenly I see it. The need to distinguish. Borne of a fear of being found out. Different. Expatriated like Wilson. Ostracised like Jean. Somehow, I could always feel it. That sense of not belonging. Of my parents being *different*. Not from here, Paris, the metropole. From a periphery that has since ceased to exist.

"But Mummy and Daddy are migrants too," Clara says, her voice loud to cover the engine. Brave little girl coming to our defence.

"It's not the same," my mother sighs. "Your mum assimilated."

I feel my shoulders drop. "How can you say that after what happened to Wilson?" I say between gritted teeth. "That word is a lie."

"Are you arguing, Mummy? I don't want you to argue," Clara says, her voice suddenly far away. Looking in the mirror I see her lower lip wobble. Turning towards her, I grasp the crunched-up ball of her fists. I can fit both of them into my palm. I force what I hope is a reassuring smile on my face and her mouth scrunches into a crooked grin. It won't be long before I can no longer contain my daughter's doubts. Soothe her fears. The reality is that her dad and I stand either side of an unspoken colour line, and that Clara will always be in the middle. I look at the rows of men sleeping rough on the pavement. It was a mistake coming to Paris to find our roots. At the end of a life that taught her the value of blending in, my mother has the luxury to pretend she believes in the lie. This won't be the case for Clara. Leandro and I will need to teach her so that she sees the world for what it is and claims her place in it.

"I tell you what, sweet pea. Shall we ring Papa and ask him when he will be home?"

"Yeah. Home! Home! Home!" Clara chants.

My mother bristles at the wheel. We drive back in silence. Coming out of the car park, she suggests we have dinner at the local Vietnamese restaurant where she introduces Clara to *nems*, shows her how to wrap them in a salad leaf and dip them in fish sauce. After a main dish of *riz cantonnais*, she orders lychees in syrup.

"Your mother's favourite when she was your age," she tells Clara, staring at me intently.

Wayfarer

The sound of water pulls me out of a deep slumber. Everything is dark at first. I notice a ray of warm light, filtering from under the closed bedroom door. Placing both feet on the ground, I stand, and walk towards the noise, reaching for the handle. The next moment, I am in a small creek, flooded with sunlight. Behind me, tree leaves rustle in the breeze. Gravel crunches underfoot. *Tout-venant* my father used to call it. The sort of gravel used in the building of Roman roads, compressed to provide a stable base under the top layers. All-who-travel. A material to facilitate movement.

A familiar groan fills the air, resonating into my bones. When I turn, Arthur is standing on the gravel as if he had been by my side all along. I feel the heat radiate from his deep fur as he approaches, nuzzling me in the direction of the river. We reach the edge of the water, shimmering in the bright sunlight. A few feet ahead is a large plank of wood floating above the current like a magic carpet. Arthur's hackles undulate as he emits a low rumble. "You want me to board the piece of wood?" I ask, understanding that somehow the bear has lost the ability to speak. I comply. As I do, I notice the raft is shaped like a door. My bedroom door. Before I can verbalise the question in my thoughts, the current takes us, lifting us, picking up speed. Past the creek we go, along a winding part of the river. The banks either side are far, the river getting wider. On land I distinguish faces coming into view. A maths teacher, a school friend, the baker. Forgotten faces making way for new ones. People I met since living in Wales. A lady with a funny hat who waves at me when walking her dog in the morning. The same *Big Issue* seller who has been sitting outside Marks & Spencer on his little foldable chair since my university days. An elderly gentleman in an oversized grey suit and muddy running trainers whom I recognise as the pensioner who feeds squirrels in the park. The barista who has been teaching me Welsh. A community of sorts.

The current is stronger now. The door jerks from side to side, bits of wood chipped off by large rocks protruding from the water. I hold on to Arthur, grabbing large clumps of his fur, remembering the day I almost drowned. Then the swirl settles and with it our floating door. I unclench my fingers, noticing a network of tributaries feeding our river into a swell. They bring other rafts carrying ethereal shapes who seem to bid us farewell. I recognise four before they dissipate into the misty air: Bonne-Maman. Jean. Max. My father. We journey on until we reach the sea, our raft feeling more stable now despite the waves. A creek comes into view and the floating door, pulled by the waves, settles onto the sand. I jump off, scanning for signs of where I might be. I spot a congregation of black rocks. Familiar ones. This is the place where Leandro and I decided to marry. Whitesands, near St Davids. I look back towards Arthur still standing on the door. Gesture for him to join me. His warm growl rolls in the air, filling my head. I understand, I tell him. Goodbye my friend.

Home

On the phone, Leandro blows raspberries to make Clara laugh but I can hear the strain in his voice. "It was brutal," he tells me once she has left the room. "The detention boat we visited was horrific. The children, Charlotte. They broke my heart."

I promise we will be home to meet him the next day and start gathering our belongings into the blue suitcase. My mother, hovering by the door to the bedroom, offers to drive us to Gare du Nord. "Sure," I say. "That would be very kind."

"Will you be back?" she asks, almost inaudible.

There is a heavy uneasiness between us.

"I don't know." In truth, I do know, with total certainty. She knows it too. "You can join us for Christmas," I offer.

"I'd like that," she replies in a long exhale.

Backtracking on ourselves, Clara and I catch the Eurostar to Euston International, making the connection to Paddington, hopping onto the Cardiff train. On board, Clara names the stations, deliberately reading each syllable. Swin-don. Rea-ding. It's like she is internally memorising our route. When we reach Bris-tol, I tell her we are only a few minutes to the tunnel that runs under the mouth of the Severn.

"To Wales!" she says, clapping her hands in excitement.

Beyond the water, I feel infused with a gradual sense of calm. I draw her attention to the familiar scenery lit up in shades of slate blue and muted greens. We marvel at the rows of redbrick houses and flashing zebra crossings which compete with large stretches of farmland, speckled with sheep, cows, and the vivid yellow of rapeseed in bloom. Above our heads, I spot a train of flying jackdaws. I remember reading that they stay in pairs for life, joined by bands of their migrating cousins from Scandinavia in the winter to form large feeding flocks.

I am French, my mother said with conviction. Do I feel so

certain? To me, identity is a treacherous construct. Beyond an accent I don't seem to be able to shake, what does it mean to be French? A certain way of seeing the world, of believing in principles of universalism and meritocracy that experience has challenged over and over again. Administrative papers that tether me to this Hexagon on which nobody in my family has had roots for at least three generations. Blood ties, maybe? Also, on a cellular level, there is nothing left of the girl who landed in Cardiff in 2001, her head filled with dreams of travel. I look at the British passport stacked on top of our train tickets; at the familiar Welsh landscape unfolding in front of our eyes; at my daughter's smile. Here, I grew, healed, had a child, dug some roots between two rivers. Here, Leandro and I found each other, two broken pots. And with the pieces we built a home. Our home.

Always yearning for something that remained out of sight, I spent too long looking back, digging into labels, only to unearth silences. Yet for all the searching, I meandered to this place, rolling, rippling, to a country of displaced pieces, like a boulder transported downriver, reshaped, smoothed into a daughter. Our daughter. Clara. I call her name, inviting her to sit by my side. "I have something for you, Clara." I pull the red leather-bound notebook out of my bag and place it into her hands.

"What is it?" she asks.

"A special book," I tell her. "Your great-uncle Jean made it for me when I was a little girl. It is a diary. A place to record secret thoughts." I point at the golden lettering on the cover. "See, he carved my name and sprinkled gold dust over the top."

Clara observes the embossed notebook on her lap with wide eyes, running the palm of her hand across the red leather. "It feels so ... old." She opens it to the first page. "Is that your handwriting, Mummy?"

"Yes, *cariad*."

She flicks through the pages, tracing the words with her finger as if practising, meandering to the point where the writing stops. She looks up. "That bit's blank."

"This is where my story ends and yours begins."

"What should I write?"

"You will know."

She nods and places the notebook in her backpack with great care.

The next moment, she is jumping from excitement on the seat opposite. "Cardiff Central is next," she says, repeating the bilingual announcement. *Caerdydd Canolog*. The horn-like sound signalling the door release makes the air vibrate. Clara presses the button as its yellow light comes on. "Mind the gap," I say, aware of the drop. Already, she is on the platform, scanning the information board.

"Platform eight," she cries, pointing at the stairs going down.

I follow her, hearing the announcement for Penarth on platform eight, Welsh phonemes echoing in my chest, both alien and familiar, like a song calling me home.

Acknowledgements

Thank you to Rebecca Parfitt for believing in this story and for Lynzie Fitzpatrick and everyone at Honno for the positive energy.

Thank you also to Richard Gwyn for sharing this meandering journey as guide and mentor.

Thank you to Jonathan, Louise, and Anthony for their time, advice, and support.

Finally, thanks and love to my Welsh family: Rhys, Théo, Seren, Bronwen, Jen, and Tony. And to my mother Danièle, for being the strongest role model a daughter could wish for. I follow in your footsteps. Merci.

Part of the chapter 'Return' was inspired by a travel writing piece I wrote as 'Revolving Doors' in *An Open Door: New Travel Writing for a Precarious Century*, edited by Steven Lovatt (Parthian, 2022).

ABOUT HONNO

Honno Welsh Women's Press was set up in 1986 by a group of women who felt strongly that women in Wales needed wider opportunities to see their writing in print and to become involved in the publishing process. Our aim is to develop the writing talents of women in Wales, give them new and exciting opportunities to see their work published and often to give them their first 'break' as a writer.

Honno is registered as a community co-operative. Any profit that Honno makes is invested in the publishing programme. Women from Wales and around the world have expressed their support for Honno. Each supporter has a vote at the Annual General Meeting. For more information and to buy our publications, please visit our website www.honno.co.uk or email us on post@honno.co.uk.

Honno
D41, Hugh Owen Building,
Aberystwyth University,
Aberystwyth,
Ceredigion,
SY23 3DY.

We are very grateful for the support of all our Honno Friends.